MAKEUP AND MOCHAS
BOOK 4

The Ride For You

NIKKI GRANT

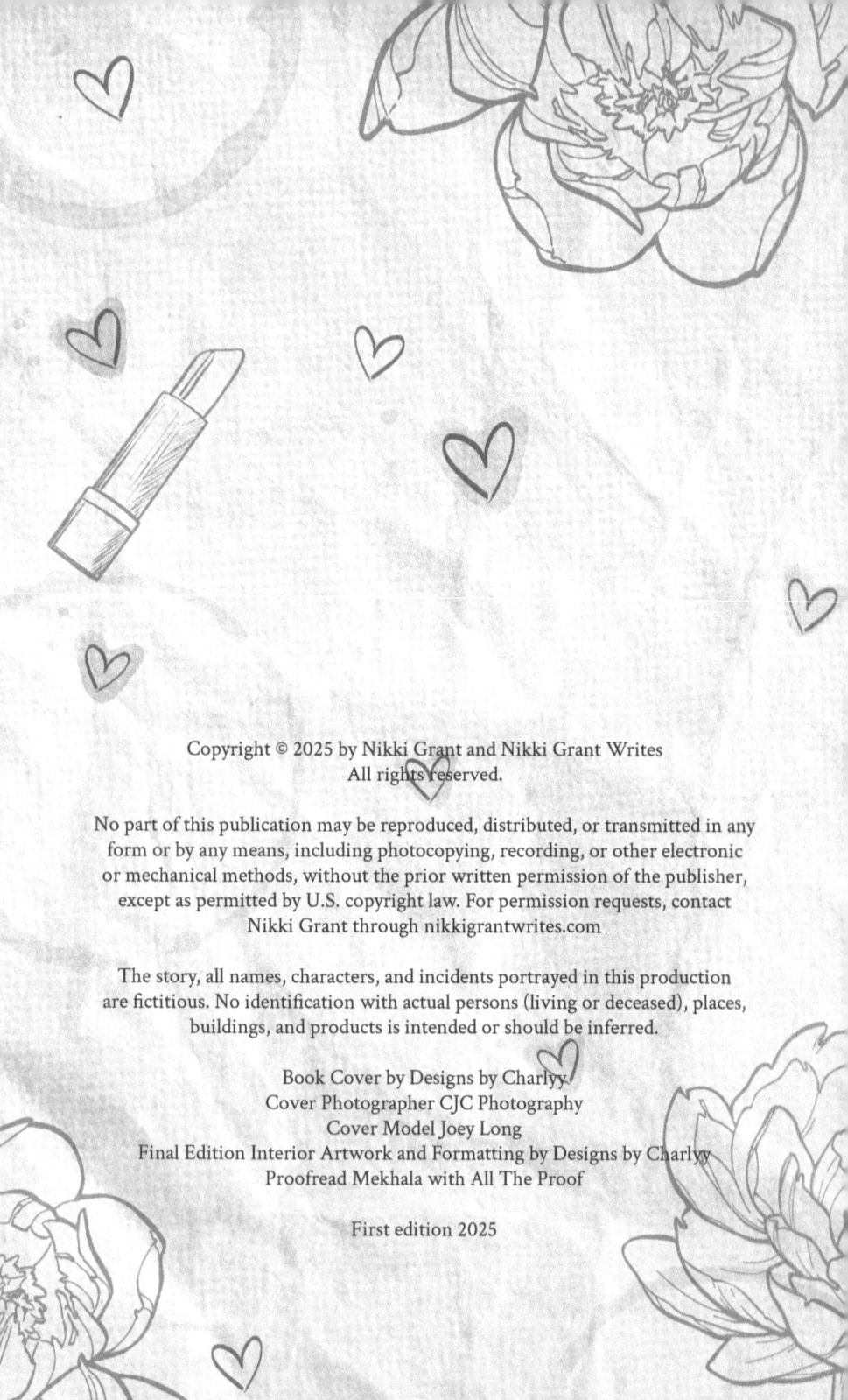

Book Cover by Designs by Charlyy
Cover Photographer CJC Photography
Cover Model Joey Long
Final Edition Interior Artwork and Formatting by Designs by Charlyy
Proofread Mekhala with All The Proof

First edition 2025

To the girls learning to ask for what they want out loud and without shame.

And knowing that one of those asks is a cozy, marriage of convenience story.
This one's for you.

LETTER FROM THE AUTHOR

I can't believe we are in the last book of the Makeup and Mochas series. When I started this journey with The Funnel to You, I never expected the conversations I would have the opportunity to share with so many of my readers. These stories have become a connection point that I never thought possible. Mental health conversations, learning to appreciate every piece of the story, and finding joy in makeup again have been just a few things that have come into my inbox over the last several months.

Every time you pick up one of these stories, you help someone else find that passion again. And now, even more of it is coming out of the page and into "for real life." I have some fun announcements coming and there's a sneak peek of just a few of those things at the end of this story. But first, enjoy the cuteness that is Jonathan and Tilly's story.

Love and sparkles,
Nikki

CHAPTER BREAKDOWN (WHERE TW AND CW HAPPEN)

Feel free to skip this page if you want to go in completely blind. This list is here for you to use as you see fit. The chapters are also listed so you can skip certain things if you want or need to.

Manipulation and negative talk from a parental figure
Ch. 1, 10, 12, 13, 16, 17, 20

Fatphobia and internal negative body talk
Ch. 4, 6, 11, 20, 23, 25

Sexually explicit scenes (kissing to more)
Ch. 21, 23, 25, 27, 28, 30

Adult language – minimal, but throughout

Alcoholic drinks
Ch. 26

Anxiety and overwhelm – minimal, but throughout
mostly internal thoughts rather than outward reactions

Tilly is a social media influencer - there is a lot of social media content throughout this book and this series. If social media content annoys you, this probably isn't the book for you. She's also an avid romance reader, so there are some references to books she's read and this book is recommended for readers over the age of eighteen as mature content is dealt with.

PLAYLIST

Crushin (feat. Lawrence) – Meghan Trainor, Lawrence
Numb Little Bug – Em Beihold
Chokehold – Austin Girogio
Fat Funny Friend – Maddie Zahm
No – Meghan Trainor
Memories – Conan Gray
Looking at Me – Sabrina Carpenter
Chasing Shadows – Alex Warren
Dandelions – Ruth B.
Highway Don't Care – Tim McGraw, Taylor Swift, Keith Urban
Daisies – Justin Beiber
ceilings – Lizzy McAlpine
Moral of the Story (feat. Niall Horan) – Ashe, Niall Horan
Honey, I'm Good – Andy Grammar
Bestie – Meghan Trainor
Burning Down – Alex Warren
It Is What It Is – Jenna Raine
22 (Taylor's Version) – Taylor Swift
Stargazing – Myles Smith
Nightlight – Livingston
Ordinary – Alex Warren
Beautiful Things – Benson Boone
Come Closer (Worship) – Nation Haven

THE RIDE FOR YOU BLOG POST #35

Surprise! I'm engaged!

I said yes to one of my best friends last night. We are planning an intimate ceremony for the end of November. My family may have wanted a big ceremony back home, but this is for the two of us and our closest friends – our chosen family.

The next few months are going to be great. Busy, but great.

Two months until we tie the knot.

Seven months until graduation.

Eight months until I start full-time at Pink Every Day.

But I'm a planner and I never shy away from a deadline. Any excuse to use my planner, highlighters, and sticky notes, and I'm a happy girl.

Now to get everything in order.

Chapter One

TILLY

FIVE YEARS AGO

MATCHA MILK TEA WITH BOBA

Social post: What has been your favorite job so far? Your girl is officially job hunting for something to do after school. If only I could be a makeup artist at fifteen... #justme #completelytilly #jobhunting #aspiringmua

Image description: Job board website with "makeup artist" in the search bar – I know it's not going to happen for a few more years, but a girl can dream.

"**T**hank you so much for your interest in the program, but we have decided to go a different way."

"We appreciate your application, but after careful consideration, we have moved forward with an applicant more in line with our goals."

"We're sorry, but..."

"After many discussions, we regret to..."

How many denial emails can I possibly receive in one day? Especially since this is literally for a part-time job after school. This isn't rocket science. I take another glance at the inbox before closing my laptop and taking a few deep breaths. I will not cry over a part-time job. They found someone else or decided to promote from within, and that's okay. The right spot is open for me. I just haven't found it yet.

I hear a door shut downstairs and decide to take my chances that it's Mom coming home and not my father. I try listening at the door, but can't tell who it is just by the movements downstairs.

"Tilly, I know you're lurking in the hallway. Come down here, I have some things I need to go over with you."

Great. Not Mom. My face immediately changes to hold a passive look. I make sure my hair isn't too out of control, and then head downstairs.

"Hi. Is this a kitchen counter conversation or an office conversation?" I ask as I grab a water bottle from the fridge. I need something to do with my hands so I don't pull on my clothes or ruin the manicure I just got done. Having unplanned conversations with Dad is never a fun time and I end up doing something to fidget to dispel the nerves. And then he notices and gives me a hard time about it – and then the conversation just goes on longer. Not fun.

"Here is fine." My father takes a moment to look me over, I'm sure searching for something he can criticize. He's only a little older than my friend's parents, but a lot more controlling. Honestly, it makes sense.

Luis Chance is not just a business owner and father, he's the mayor. And because of that, I don't get to *just* be a teenage girl. Nope. I have to be the picture-perfect mayor's daughter. Not gonna lie, it sucks.

I sit on one of the stools at the kitchen island and wait for him to continue. I may be getting impatient, but I can't let him know that. Forcing myself to become comfortable with the silence he's dragging out, I count the speckles of white confetti type dots on my jeans instead of seeking to fill the silence. I don't need another lecture today about being a "proper young lady."

"I know you have been wanting to get a job after school, but you are much better spending your time on your studies, or working on office tasks, if you are really wanting something official. You don't need to be working at a coffee shop or a retail establishment. That won't serve you now or in your future." The disappointment he has in me is palpable. No surprise there.

"How do you know I'm applying for jobs?" I make sure to keep my voice even in tone, even though I feel like I could scream at him for trying to control yet another area of my life.

He just looks at me like I should know the answer to this. "Anyway, how are your classes going? Have you decided on an undergrad program yet, so we can begin working on those applications?" Okay, subject changed.

"I think I want to go into aesthetics – specifically makeup and skincare. There's been a lot of advancements in product efficacy and ingredients lately, and it is absolutely fascinating." I'm about to pull up a new study on my phone when I hear my dad chuckling.

"Oh, you're serious." His grin falls when he makes eye contact with me. "Tilly, that's not happening. You have a role in this family and this community. I was thinking event planning or campaign coordination, or even copywriting. You aren't going to be able to play around with makeup all day. Jason's father and I have been talking about what things look like for your future and his expectations of our family." I don't let him continue with that line of conversation.

"Expectations? What expectations? Why are you talking to my boyfriend's father about any of this?"

"Tilly, we've talked about this. You and Jason are getting married once you are twenty-two. And then we will be able to continue working on the city initiatives together, as a family unit. You haven't had a problem with this before."

"Jason is nice and all, but he's literally my first boyfriend. In name, more than anything else. I don't even know the last time he texted me outside of arranging to pick me up for the dinner you hosted last month. He doesn't love me, and I've seriously been thinking about calling things off. I don't need a boyfriend right now. I want to enjoy being a teenager and playing with things like makeup and skincare, and clothes. You signed up for a life of politics, I didn't." I slide off the stool and start toward my room.

"Tilly," my dad calls after me. I take a deep breath and turn to face him. "You will do this. It's not up for discussion. I'll have a list of acceptable colleges and universities for you to apply to by the end of next week. And you will not break things off with Jason. Is that understood?"

"Tilly, I don't understand why you're making such a big deal about this. It's important to our parents, and it's not like we have to get married tomorrow." Jason sits next to me in the car while he drives us to school the next day. I thought he'd have my back on this, but apparently, he's totally fine following everything our dads have planned for our lives.

"I know that. But is this seriously what you want? To take over the business for your dad and build a modern-day empire in small-town USA? Because that's not what I want." I stare out the window, trying to rein in my emotions. I will not cry in front of him. My makeup looks too good to cry it all off before we even get to school. I feel his hand resting on my thigh, and I force myself to sit still and not shove him off me.

"And you're calling makeup a better career choice? I'm not going to make you stop playing with the makeup and skincare stuff, Tilly. But we need to make a plan that aligns with our parents' wishes and our own goals, too." I don't respond. I don't know how, and I know I'm not winning this argument today. Sometimes it's just easier to sit still and listen. It's not worth the fight.

I stay quiet for days, weeks, and months. I didn't want to cause a scene. I didn't want to upset anyone. It was easier to go with the flow. I applied to colleges, I went to events, and I tried to be who my dad needed me to be. And all the while, I hated it. I didn't want to have this life. I was miserable, but I had to look a certain way on the outside. After all, Dad was a public figure, which meant I was a public figure too. Yes, even at sixteen. It wasn't until my mom pulled me aside a few weeks after my sixteenth birthday that I realized I may have another option here.

"I've been talking to your dad about the extra pressure he's been putting on you." I went to interrupt her to try to tell her I was okay, but she put a hand up to stop me. "I know you're trying to do everything he is asking of you, but it's not fair to ask so much of his teenage daughter. I've convinced your dad to let us try something else for a little while."

"Something else? Like what?"

"How do you feel about moving to Colorado?"

Chapter Two

TILLY

PRESENT DAY

Cherry Green Tea

Social Post: It's almost time for the craziness of a new semester, which means I get to go pick out a new tea. Necessary? No. Still gonna happen? Absolutely. #csusenior #coloradocolleges #allthetea #completelytilly #finalyear

Image Description: Photo of the outside of the tea house in Old Town Fort Collins.

Senior year starts tomorrow, and my emotions couldn't be more mixed. On the one hand, I am literally months away from my dream job – working as the marketing director for Pink Every Day. I've seen this company start from day one until where it's grown to today. And now I'm this close to fully being on the payroll full-time, in a leadership position no less. And it's not just a makeup company – it's a space to help other woman-owned businesses thrive. A place of innovation and connection, and yes, some really amazing makeup too. But that's just one possible outcome for me by the end of this school year.

If my dad has his wish, I'll not be graduating. I'll end out this year with my MRS degree and nothing else. When Mom and I left home several years ago, it was under the expectation that I would be able to live my life how I saw fit. Mom would be there to support me and help me make decisions and be a young adult. But Dad would have no say in things. To the public, Mom was coming out here with me to take care of her elderly parents. We made visits back home for the holidays, but that was it. And it's been amazing. But I knew this couldn't last forever.

Apparently, my lovely father signed an actual contract a few years ago. Who even does that? Luis Chance – literally just him. So, unless I want to "ruin his reputation" and "hurt any chances of a respectable career," my time here is almost up. Part of me hates that I haven't told my friends about any of this. But if I didn't talk about it, then it wasn't a real-life actual problem that I'd have to deal with. Procrastination and hiding from problems are okay, right? Wrong. Because now the clock is ticking. And it's only a matter of days before Dad calls in and demands I come home.

I might as well enjoy this while it lasts.

My best friend, Ashley, graduated last semester, so it's just me and Corinne on campus now. Luckily, Ashley doesn't live far away, and Pink Every Day has offices close to the CSU campus. After getting settled into my new dorm room and finishing up the final touches in the space, I decide to head to the store to grab some new tea before downtown gets too busy. Old Town Fort Collins has become one of my favorite places, but it's definitely the place to be in the evening. With all of the restaurants and shops available, it's not hard to find something to do. The only thing hard to find is a close parking space to whatever the chosen activity is. My favorite part is that the Old Town area has two tea shops that offer a wonderful variety of leaves and blends.

Sasha is the owner of Pink Every Day, and that girl has made coffee her entire personality. Ashley is her fiancé's younger sister, and she's also addicted to coffee drinks and coffee shops. Me, on the other hand? I don't actually like coffee. I know, that's practically heresy. But it's true. To me, preparing a cup of tea is an art form, and I love all the different stories and backgrounds that come from the cultures that have tea as a central part of their tradition. And I've made it a point at the beginning of each semester to come to one of the tea houses and pick out my blend for that semester. Something special that I can look forward to after a hard day or during study sessions. Now to see which one speaks to me for my last few months of freedom. Am I being a bit overdramatic? Yes. Am I going to curb that? Not at all.

The tea shop is filled with an eclectic mix of people. Grandmothers picking up a refill on their favorite black teas, moms and daughters looking at the new fruit blends for tea parties, and those like me who read the stories and intentions behind each blend. I greet the lady behind the counter and make my way over to the wall of green teas and curated blends on one of the walls.

There have been a few new ones added to the selection since the last time I was in here, so I take my time looking over the options. I pick up a pack of the Cherry Green Tea to look closer at the origin of the leaves and the notes that the tea house put on it, when I hear a familiar, yet unexpected, voice behind me.

"I'm not really sure what I need. He just asked that I pick up something that would be a dark pink color. Not purple, not red, not orange. It has to be a true pink." I spin around and have to hold back a laugh. Jonathan looks so out of place in here. His jeans still have grease stains on them, showing he was probably working under a car earlier today. At least his hands and shirt are clean. His hair looks like he's been running his fingers through it for the majority of the day, though. And the sales associate looks mildly offended that he is asking for a color of tea and not an actual variety. I walk over to rescue him and try to figure out what on earth he needs pink tea for.

"Maybe I can help?" I offer as I walk into his line of sight. It takes him just a moment to recognize me, and he visibly relaxes. It's tea, why is he so tense? Jonathan is one of Matt's best friends. Matt is Sasha's fiancé and Ashley's older brother. The two of us haven't exactly hung out or talked at length, but we've been at the same events quite a few times over the last few years. Honestly, I've had a hard time knowing how to act around him before. Nervousness isn't usually something I deal with, except around him.

"Oh, thanks, Tilly. Luca sent me down here to get a few new teas. He's finishing up another project and wants to get some wood staining so he can be ready for the next commissioned piece. But he didn't actually know what he needed. I figured it would be pretty straightforward to find a pink tea, but none of these actually look pink." He trails off while his eyes look at the wall of tea behind me. He almost looks like a lost puppy, and it's kind of cute.

"What kind of wood is he working with this time?" I ask to get some information so I know what kind of pink we need to be looking for. I'm not sure I'll know exactly what the right one will be, but I can definitely try.

"Pine, so a lighter color wood. It's for a nursery, I think, so he just wants to add a light pink shade to it without any heavy chemicals. So here we are." He motions to the wall of teas, and I giggle at his overwhelmed expression.

"Okay, let's take a look at some options." I bring him over to the fruit blends to show him the ones I think would work best. I don't miss the shake of the employees' head as she walks away, absolutely befuddled by this man. He listens like I'm going to quiz him on this later. Jonathan is always so confident in every interaction I've seen him in before. But it's refreshing to see that he doesn't act like he knows everything all the time. We finally settled on a hibiscus blend and a pomegranate blend for him to bring back to Luca. And I have another two teas in my own basket too. Plus, a new glass teapot. It's so pretty and I can't wait to use it! Pretty for content and functional too – that's a winner for sure.

"Thanks for your help in there. I was incredibly overwhelmed and had no clue where to start looking for what Luca needed."

Jonathan holds the door open for me as we head outside with our bags of carefully selected items.

"It's not a problem. But now you owe me the next time my car makes a funny noise." Jonathan laughs before composing himself enough to respond.

"You know I do body work, not mechanics, right?"

"I thought you did mechanics too."

"I do, but it's not my focus. Depending on what the noise is, I won't be your best option for help. But I'm happy to do what I can." I get to said vehicle and put my bag on the passenger seat before turning back to Jonathan, still standing on the sidewalk in front of my car.

"Thanks for that. This one's still in pretty good shape, but I'll let you know if something comes up. I'll see you at the wedding?"

"Yeah, see you at the wedding."

Sasha and Matt are getting married in a little over a month, and now I'm picturing Jonathan's broad muscles in a tailored suit. Okay then, this is gonna be awkward if I don't say goodbye like right now.

"Bye, Jonathan," I offer an awkward wave and then get in my car. And he doesn't walk away until I safely pull out into traffic.

13

- June

- Wednesday

2:00 *tail light replacement*

165 201

- Week · 24

04:46 · 21:10
01:15 · **24**

- July

Chapter Three

JONATHAN

STRAWBERRY OAT SMOOTHIE

Social Post: Throwback photo to one of my favorite cars I've had the pleasure of working on so far. This Corvette is a classic! And yes, she's more than a garage trophy. #autobodywork #classiccars #carrestoration #masterscarrestoration

Image Description: Photo of the 1973 C3 Corvette from a previous restoration project on the lot at Masters Car Restoration. Body work completed by Jonathan Masters, Owner.

Tilly is the most beautiful woman I have ever seen in my life. The curves, her smile, the way her entire face lights up when she is excited about something. I have to force myself to speak coherently every single time I interact with her. There have definitely been some times over the years that I've known her that I just sit back to watch her work with the girls in the group and see the way she so easily connects with everyone

around her. Sometimes, there's been a feeling of almost annoyance on my end because I wasn't the one getting the attention. Childish, I know. Which is why I kept my mouth shut and just watched. Maybe now I can actually talk to her like a competent adult and not a star-struck teenage boy.

She's at least six inches shorter than me, and having her stand next to me while looking at the teas today really showed off that height difference. I had to reach for a few of the blends for her while she was talking about the different options. I didn't realize there was so much to know about tea. But I guess she probably would be surprised about the types of paint and surface finishes that I have available for the cars I work on. We each have our passions. And this one is definitely one of hers.

After checking out and walking her outside, I make sure she gets on her way, and then I head over to my own car to take the fifteen-minute drive to Luca's house. He's working in the garage on his project, and his girlfriend Kylie is sitting out there with him, sketching in her project notebook.

"Not that I mind running these errands for you, but why was *I* the one tasked with picking out tea for your new staining project?" I ask Luca as I set the bag next to him on the work table. He finishes sanding the piece he's working on before setting the tools down to look at me.

"Kylie just got home from a consultation, and you were already out that way anyway." Luca shrugs like it's obvious. "Besides, it helps to get new perspectives on stuff when it comes to creative pieces. What did you get?" He wipes off his hands to rid them of the excess sawdust before he opens the bag in front of him.

"Luckily, Tilly was there to help me pick these out because I couldn't figure out which teas would stain pink enough to show up. And the worker acted like no one had ever asked her about creating wood stains with tea before. She was actually pretty offended when I asked about the color of the tea rather than the variety." Kylie doesn't even try to subdue her laughter at my expense. It was an awkward encounter, and she knows it. At least Luca tries to muffle his laugh before he sets the bag down again.

"Tilly was there? That's random. When do classes start for her?"

Kylie finally gets out once she stops laughing long enough to take a breath.

"Uh, I'm not sure. She mentioned picking out her semester blends. So, I guess she's in there pretty often. I didn't realize she liked tea that much. That girl can talk about tea." I smirk and shake my head a bit as I remember how in-depth she got in talking about the different types of teas and some of the history behind the ones we inevitably chose.

"There's that smile again. I swear you like that girl. Every time her name gets brought up or you see her, you get that look in your eye," Luca teases and I quickly school my expression.

"What look? I don't know what you're talking about."

"The one where you pretend you haven't already fallen for her."

"So, what are we working on this time?" I ask one of my regulars as he comes into the waiting room at the shop. I've worked on five of Clark's cars over the years, and each one has been a new challenge. They've all been classic cars that have needed anywhere between full restoration to minor body work. With classic cars, most of the time anyway, the owners want them to be restored like they were in their original condition. And that's what Clark likes for his, so the expectations are pretty straightforward when he brings me a new vehicle.

"I got another Mustang for you. Looking to restore to sell this one. I worked with a new broker for it to get the work done and there's a businessman that has already purchased it pending work completion. If you can take a look and give me an estimate, then we can get it scheduled depending on what's needed."

"Sounds good. Do you want to wait while I take a look, or are you dropping it off?" I pull out his file and make a few notes before passing the paperwork over to him to finish filling out.

"Dropping off, Maggie's in her car waiting for me. We're going to grab lunch, and I can come back and get it? Unless you think it'll take a while, then I can come back tomorrow?"

"Lunch should be good. I'm still waiting on the paint to dry down on the only other car in the shop today, so I'll be able to get right on this one." Clark gives me a wave and then heads out to his wife's 1976 C3 Corvette that I fixed up for him last year. That car is still one of my favorites, out of everything I've ever worked on, and I'm glad it's with someone who appreciates it.

When I get outside to look at the new acquisition in Clark's garage, I have to hold back a legit fist pump in excitement. This man just made my entire day. The 1968 Shelby Mustang GT500 KR sitting in front of me isn't just a classic car; it's one of the most sought-after classic cars out there. Most of these go for well over 100k. And I get to work on one.

After going through my routine inspection and filling out my estimate sheet, I head back inside to start looking up parts, paint, and the original specs of the vehicle. This is the part of the job that I don't enjoy quite as much. But my office manager has the day off, so it's on me. I can have the full quote done for Clark by the time he gets back. Luckily, the car is already in fairly great condition. But this is my area of expertise, and my dream car. So, we aren't going to be cutting any corners when it comes to this one.

"What's the damage?" Clark asks as he walks back into my office about an hour later.

"Not that bad actually. We're looking at 10k for parts and labor. Not sure on the mechanical side of things, but that's for the interior, exterior, and touch-ups. I can get someone in here to do a work up on mechanics next week if that works for your schedule. Do you have a deadline on when it needs to be done for the buyer?" I hand over the paperwork so he can see the workup.

"Yeah, it's some guy out of Chicago. I need to finalize everything, but it looks like he's giving it to his business partner at the end of the year as a gift for closing out some contracts. It needs to be done by December 21st if we can make that happen."

Seems like a pretty big gift for some contracts, but okay, to each their own. "I'll see what getting the pieces and paint look like and will let you know tomorrow when I can expect to start working on it."

"And this is why I come to you. Thanks, Jonathan."

There's something about starting a new project. Getting into a new vehicle and seeing what needs to happen to bring it back to life, back to what it was originally created to be. Don't get me wrong, I like working on new cars and custom projects. But the restorations are what bring me joy. It's what I'm good at. And I can't wait to start working on Clark's newest acquisition. But first, I need to pick up a new vehicle in Montana. I've worked with this buyer before, so I was thrilled when he called and asked if I'd be able to pick up the car and work on it for him. He's in Europe for another six weeks, and he doesn't trust anyone else to drive it. No complaints here.

I just hate doing these trips by myself. I'd ask Matt to come, but he's getting married soon. And Luca is in the middle of a project he can't walk away from, plus Kylie has had more flair ups recently than normal, and I hate to ask him to leave her when she needs his support. I'm still mulling over my options when I get an Instagram notification. They don't pop up often, but I do have an account for the shop. I welcome the distraction instead of ignoring it. Figuring out the logistics of the Montana trip isn't going to be solved while I count the wooden planks on the floor of my office.

@completelytilly: Hi Jonathan, I hope it's okay to message you here. I realized I didn't have your phone number when I pulled out my phone earlier. And I know you probably keep this channel just for work stuff. But this is kind of work stuff, maybe?

@masterscarrestoration: It's no problem, Tilly. What's going on?

@completelytilly: My car just totally died on the side of the road, and I didn't know who else to call. Sasha and Ashley are in Denver today, and Kylie is in the middle of a PCOS flair up, so she's stuck in bed today waiting that out.

@masterscarrestoration: Where are you?

@completelytilly: I was just leaving Ulta in Fort Collins, so I'm on the side of the road on 287, heading north toward campus.

@masterscarrestoration: I'm on my way.

Fifteen minutes later, I pull up behind Tilly's little Honda Civic. It's an older model, but these cars hold up really well. It shouldn't have just died on her. I throw on my hazard lights before carefully making my way over to the passenger side of her car. She's engrossed in her phone, so she doesn't see my walk up, which is clear when I tap on her window and she screams, tossing her phone in the process. Her face turns bright red in embarrassment, and I have to hold back a laugh. She's cute when she's flustered.

Tilly presses a button on the door, and I hear the locks click. Opening the door, I kneel down a bit so I can talk to her through the open space.

"You called?"

Chapter Four

TILLY

CHAI PROTEIN SMOOTHIE

Social Post: Tea has been purchased, new notebooks are prepped, now I just need a new lippie for the semester. Yes, I am that girl. Quick, help me pick!! #makeupshopping #lippie #completelytilly #ultafinds #fallmakeup

Image Description: My hand holding three new lip stains from a Colorado based company because you can never have too many pink lipsticks and these shades are gorgeous!!

If this ends up being something stupid like I went too long before an oil change, I'll literally die of embarrassment. I know I'm over on the scheduled and recommended maintenance dates, but I didn't think my car would throw an actual fit over my lack of attention. I've been a little busy pretending my dad isn't trying to figure out a way to get me to come back home by really focusing on prepping for classes to start, wedding stuff for Sasha, and the pieces of Pink Every Day that I get to have a hand in already.

So, I'm totally zoned out, staring at my phone, when a light knock on my passenger window scares the absolute everything out of me. Obviously, I scream and throw my phone. And then cringe and hope I didn't just break it. I don't have the money to fix that right now. And I'll sell feet pics before I ask my father for help. Not that I think it's beneath me to sell feet pics, but I'm not a little woman, and my feet aren't exactly getting model requests. I finally manage to get the doors to unlock, and Jonathan pokes his head inside the car.

"You called?" His smirk has me smiling back at him and trying to settle my heart from the imminent threat of danger his knocking had scared me into thinking.

"Hey, yeah. Thanks for coming." I move to get out of the car, but he grabs my arm before I can open the door. I go to protest, but then feel how close a speeding car is to my own vehicle as it passes by.

"Well, that definitely wasn't the speed limit." I chuckle, trying to dispel my growing anxiety in this situation. I'm stranded on the side of the road. I'm hot and sweaty from nerves and frustration and the fact that it's literally one hundred degrees outside. And Jonathan is touching me. In a possessive, 'I've got you' kind of way, but still.

"Probably not," he smiles, then looks outside again before nodding at me, indicating that it's finally safe to leave the car. I do so very slowly, hoping that the drivers will respect that I'm getting out of my car and joining Jonathan on the sidewalk. I hand him my keys and let out an exasperated sigh.

"I don't know what happened. All the lights blinked on the dashboard, and then I had enough time to pull over before everything just stopped. I hate to bother you, but I didn't know who else to call. My mom is with her parents today, too."

"Car problems don't wait for it to be convenient, unfortunately. They're related to printers in that way. Let me see what I can figure out. Go sit in my car so you can get in the AC. There's a water bottle in there, too, that you can grab."

"Oh, it's no problem. I want to help. What can I do?" The

answering smile he gives me has all kinds of flutters happening in my belly and more heat rushing to my cheeks. And he definitely notices the latter. He's too polite to tell me that I won't be able to help him with checking out the car.

"I've got this, Tilly. Go sit. Take a breath. This stuff is stressful, and you're allowed to go rest for a minute. Let me be your knight in shining armor." I smile at his response and reluctantly go sit in his car, which has working A.C. and a bottle of water waiting for me, just like he said. This is nice! I have no clue what kind of car this is, but it's obvious this man likes good vehicles. It still smells new!

Ten minutes later, Jonathan slips into the driver's side, grabbing a rag from the middle console and wiping something gross off his hands before pulling out his phone. I let him finish what he is doing before I ask what he thinks happened.

"So, how bad is it?"

"I think it probably just overheated. You're nearly completely out of coolant and are overdue for an oil change. I could get the electrical systems to turn on, but the engine isn't turning over. I'll come back and get it once it cools down outside. I may need to tow it to my buddy's shop or have him come take a look over at mine. This is more his area of expertise, and I think you need a bit more work done than just the oil change."

The noise I make as I let my head fall back on the headrest is definitely not lady-like, but this sucks. I don't have the time or money for this. *I could have the money for this*, a quiet inner voice reminds me. Yeah, but then I would have to talk to my dad, and that's not happening before I absolutely have to. I can do this adulting thing on my own. Without him. I'm a competent adult. I can do this. I don't realize how in my head I am until I feel a hand rest on my thigh. I open my eyes to glance down at the contact and then at Jonathan.

"You okay? You kind of zoned out on me there for a minute. Do you need another bottle of water?" The concern on his face is evident, and I hate that I just totally freaked him out, again.

"Yeah, just trying to figure out all the logistics and costs for this. I think I can put the tow on my credit card if they can wait until Friday. I get paid on Thursday from some work I did for a friend's social media accounts earlier this month. And then, I can call an Uber to get back to campus. Luckily, I don't have to leave campus much for the next two weeks. That should buy us enough time to figure out what's happening. Right?" I hope I'm right. Please say I'm right.

His smile is reassuring, "This isn't going to be too much work, Tilly. Don't stress over this. How about you pay me back by assisting me with something else?"

"Like what? Your social media and website are already in great shape, I don't think I could do much with that…" I trail off, honestly not knowing what I could possibly help him with. But it seems like he already has something in mind.

"Classes don't start until next week, right?" I nod. "Come with me to pick up a car in Montana? I don't want to make the drive by myself. I'd be driving, but having someone to talk to helps make it not as long of a trip."

"That hardly seems like an even trade for all the parts and labor. I don't even know how to estimate what that would look like. There's no way that's fair to you."

"You'll be doing me a favor. Trust me. I don't want to make that drive by myself. We'd need to fly out tomorrow morning if possible, and then we'd pick up the car in the afternoon. The guy that has the car wants it off his lot, so I unfortunately don't have a ton of time to plan out all the logistics. I'd see how far we could get before we would need to stop for a few hours to rest and eat. And then we'd finish the drive on the second day. Not a long trip, but I really hate doing road trips by myself." He's laying it on thick and I have to smile at the way he's trying to convince me that this is a good idea.

I know I'm staring. How on earth is this a fair trade? But he's given me no reason not to believe what he's saying. I can text Sasha when I get back to my room to make sure this isn't totally insane. But even if it is, my time for crazy ideas is running out.

"Well, you better get me back to my dorm then so I can pack a bag."

Am I nuts for agreeing to an impromptu road trip literally days before classes start? I didn't think so. But, waking up to the 4:00 alarm this morning has me questioning my choices. Jonathan had texted me flight information last night and that he'd be here to get me at five this morning. Gross. Who does that? Anyway, I said okay, so here we are. I take a quick shower and then throw my things in an overnight bag. We're only planning on taking two days to get back, so I'm not going with the bigger of my suitcases. I also don't want to have to check anything. Leggings, an oversized tee, and comfy shoes tie off the look for the morning. It's before the sun wakes up, so I'm not stressing about being too cute this morning. Comfy and confident. That's the vibe for the day. Add a pop of lip gloss and I'm all set.

I barely emember to grab a sweatshirt before heading down to the dorm's lobby. It's going to be freezing on the airplane. And in the car, depending on how Jonathan likes to road trip. I feel the buzz of my phone vibrating just as I get downstairs, and am not at all surprised to see Jonathan's pretty car just outside. I really need to figure out what he drives because it is a very pretty car and I'm sure it has an actual name and not just "pretty." And he obviously loves it because it's immaculate inside. Like, I could eat off the floor levels of clean. Not that I would, that's weird. Anyway, he's here. So, I don't have to wait around for too long. *Yay me.*

"Good morning," he greets in that gravelly voice that guys have in the morning. He offers to take my bag and sets it on the back seat next to his own. As I get settled into the passenger seat, I notice that he already has the seat warmer going. Okay, this guy pays attention to the little things. Nice.

"That second cup is for you, by the way. I wasn't sure what you liked to drink, but figured starting the morning off with a chai protein smoothie would be a safe bet since I saw you in the tea shop. Let me know what you think." He smiles at me before leaving the parking lot. I take a sip and am surprised by how good it is. Most of the time, protein shakes are chalky and gross, but this is amazing.

"Did you make this?" I take another sip, reminding myself not to drink too fast. It's a little over an hour to the airport, and I don't need to ask for a potty break before we get there.

"Yeah. Matt and Sasha have the full coffee set up at their place, Kylie and Luca have tea, Marcus and Ashley have a mix of both – and I have a little bit of everything for the hot drinks, plus a full smoothie and juicing bar."

"Smoothies and juicing? Are you a secret gym rat or something? Wait, is that an okay thing to say or is that offensive? I am so sorry. Please tell me I didn't just totally cross a line." I can't help the giggle that comes out at the mix of shock and then embarrassment at my initial response. I didn't expect that from him. This man is covered in grease and paint more days than not, at least from what I can remember. I don't see him as a green-juice sipping kind of guy.

"Not really," he laughs out in his response. "I like playing around with the different benefits of fresh juices and then herbs that I add them to my smoothies. And I know you like tea, so I found a recipe for a chai smoothie that also worked with a protein mix I had at the house. So, it's breakfast and a little bit of caffeine, but it's also got enough in there that we should be good until lunchtime. Or we can stop and get food once we get to our destination. No worries either way."

"Wow, that was unexpected. But that's cool. Cars and chai – you do it all."

"I'll have to add that to my Instagram bio."

13

• June

• Wednesday

2:00 tail light replacement

185-201

• Week - 24

04:46 🔆 21:10
01:15 🌙 24

July

Chapter Five

JONATHAN

JAMBA JUICE APPLES 'N GREENS ™

Social Post: Sometimes a car needs to be picked up before work can be completed. Some car owners choose to have the vehicle transported through a service, but sometimes, I get to go pick them up myself. #roadtrip #masterscarrestoration #newproject #nococars

Image Description: Airport Terminal at Denver International Airport

So, Tilly may not have been the best choice for a travel companion. First, she fell asleep on the eighty-minute drive to the airport. Granted, it's early in the morning, and I didn't give her a lot of notice on this, but she passed out shortly after finishing her smoothie. At least she liked it. I hope she wasn't just getting it down to appease me. But I don't see her as someone who would tell me she liked something when she doesn't.

Secondly, she smells way too good in this confined space. And

I have to keep reminding myself that she's a friend, a drop-dead gorgeous friend, but a friend. And I cannot go there with her. We don't know each other that well. Not well enough for me to ask her out at six in the morning anyway. And I've never seen her show anyone interest. She seems to be the kind of girl who is focused on her career and her friends. Come to think of it, I don't know much about her personal life outside of the fact that her mom is the only one here with her. But her mom stays with her parents more often than not, while Tilly stays on campus.

She's a senior this year and will be working at Pink Every Day with Sasha and Ashley. She likes tea. Her hair is the perfect shade of brown that has its own story of highlights, showcasing how much she loves the sun. And the freckles on her nose are still visible from the summer. I don't get to see her much without makeup on, but seeing her sleeping on the seat next to me...she's stunning.

And I'm in trouble if I think I'm going to get through the next forty-eight hours without telling her that.

Chapter Six

TILLY

PINEAPPLE GINGER GREEN SMOOTHIE

*Social Post: Airport and road trip fit. Last minute trips mean comfort,
but still something I feel cute in. When you travel do you go for cute or
comfort? Or both? #travelday #roadtripping #justme #mirrorselfie*

*Image Description: Full-body OOTD picture of me in the airport
bathroom. Super chic, I know.*

Falling asleep in the car? Not awful.
Waking up to realize I literally drooled all over the leather
seat and the shoulder of my sweater? Kill. Me. Now.

Not really, but ugh, that's embarrassing. Granted, the sun is
only now coming up, and we just got to the airport. I really hope
this dries soon because it's obvious that I drooled all over myself in
the car. *Nice one, Tilly.*

Jonathan finds a parking space in the attached lot to the airport
and then grabs both of our bags before we head into the terminal.
Luckily, it isn't too busy for the first thing in the morning. The

Denver airport is super-efficient with how they run things, but it can be overwhelming when you first get inside the terminal. Since we don't have to check bags, we make our way right to security.

I am so glad that I layered up this morning, though, because it is frigid in here! Okay, it's probably a comfortable temperature for normal people, but I'm cold. I know they say that bigger girls are never cold, but my body missed that memo. I don't complain out loud though because Ashley literally has an autoimmune disease that makes her cold, and I don't have that. I just have a hard time regulating my temperature. Especially after I've been sleeping. And of course, security asks me to take off my sweatshirt. Gotta love showing off all the belly rolls through my tank top first thing in the morning.

Don't get me wrong, I love my curves. I love my body and all the space I take up. But I still notice the looks from people when they think I'm not in good shape or I'm not taking care of myself. There are definitely still some days that I envy Ashley and Sasha and how easily they can find cute clothes that fit them. And days when I wish I didn't have the memories of being teased and taunted in junior high and high school. I wasn't the cheerleader. I wasn't the homecoming queen. I was the quiet daughter of a very vocal mayor. One who had her whole life planned out for her. And finally got tired of never having a say.

Now, here we are.

When I retrieve my sweatshirt and put it back on the other side of the pat down, I'm not surprised to see Jonathan staring. The security agent wasn't exactly quiet with her disdain for the additional work I was causing her. I'm not going to apologize for it though. It's her job and I didn't do anything wrong. What I wasn't expecting, though, was the heat I see in his eyes. For me? No, that can't be right. I need more caffeine, and apparently, he does too, because there's no way this gorgeous man in front of me sees me as anything other than a friend.

Right?

By the time we find our gate and put eyes on it to make sure it's actually real, we only have thirty minutes until boarding begins. (Don't act like you don't do it too.) I double check the boarding time again and then excuse myself to go the restroom, and Jonathan makes his way down to the breakfast places past this section of gates. He's probably going to grab some coffee. I should go find some caffeine, too. Or maybe I'll wait until we get to our destination. I'm not sure if he's going to ask me to drive at all. Probably not the best idea to give me the keys, but I'm glad to be a passenger princess. And this is a client car, anyway, so I shouldn't be driving it.

"The paper towels are out," a lady at the sink next to me says as soon as I finish washing my hands in the bathroom.

"Oh, that's unfortunate." Now to decide if I'm going to wipe my hands on my leggings or shake them out. Why does this bathroom have no air dryer things? So weird. I decide to shake them off a bit and then make my way back to the gate. I need to chill for a bit before getting shoved into a small space with a whole bunch of people. I don't generally deal with anxiety, not like Sasha does anyway. But it's still something that happens when I'm in a new situation, or feeling rushed, or in crowded spaces. Okay, maybe anxiety is something I deal with more than I thought I did. I need to talk to Sasha about this. Adding that to the mental to-do list. Jonathan meets me at our gate again, and I immediately start blushing because I was off in my own thoughts, and he was just waiting for me to make eye contact to start talking to me. Apparently he learned from the phone throwing incident in the car yesterday.

"I wasn't sure what your usual drink order was, so I just grabbed you what I normally get for myself. I can go get you something else if this grosses you out." Jonathan passes me a white Styrofoam cup as I settle into the seat next to him. I recognize the smoothie logo on the side and smile.

"You must really like smoothies?" I chuckle at him. I did not picture this guy as a health nerd, but it's kind of cute.

"Eh, it's a good way to get a lot of productive calories and fruits and veggies without sitting down and eating at every meal and snack time. There are days that I don't stop long enough to prepare meals and cook, so this is a way I can make sure I still take care of myself while fulfilling work obligations." His answer is straightforward and isn't condescending in any way. Some people love finding those little ways to hint that I'm fat and therefore, not taking care of myself, whenever they can. And Jonathan hasn't done that. And it's kind of a nice reprieve.

"That makes sense. I tend to forget to eat, too. And then I survive on fruit snacks and granola bars until Ashley or someone else makes me sit down and eat. I've always been that way, honestly." I take a sip of the smoothie and have to hold back a little happy dance. "This is so good, what the heck is this?" I force myself to sip slowly so I don't give myself brain freeze. That would just be so attractive next to my drool-stained shoulder.

The chuckle next to me causes a blush to hit my cheeks again, and I don't try to hide it this time. "It's just an apple and greens blend. It's a good morning one, and close to one I make at home a few times a week. It's even kid-approved, so it's one I keep ready often."

"Do you have a couple of kids I don't know about?"

"Not yet. I watch my sister's kids a couple of mornings a week and then bring them to school. She and her husband's work schedules let them be home every night for dinner and home on the weekends, but mornings are a little harder. They live just a couple of streets over, so they bring the boys over on Tuesdays and Fridays. I do breakfast and then bring them to school by eight. And then I still have time to get into the shop by nine when we fully open up. It works." He smiles at me like this wasn't brand new information. What guy in his mid-twenties is just that good with kids?

"How old are they?" I try to keep the conversation going. If nothing else, being the daughter of a politician means that I'm really good at keeping the conversation focused on whoever I'm talking to. It's almost a reflex for me at this point.

"Six and eight. My sister is a little older than me, and they started their family pretty fast after making it official. And I get to be the uncle that sneaks in veggies when they aren't looking. So, my sister lets me be the fun uncle." I don't miss the wink he sends my way, and I can feel my cheeks heating again. Why am I blushing so much around this man? I don't get embarrassed easily. But I'm not expecting him to turn the conversation back on me. Most people like talking about themselves. But Jonathan is quick to turn it back.

"What about you? Any siblings or nieces or nephews?"

"Um, nope. Just me. My dad has always been pretty busy, and my mom worked alongside him. So, I was a nanny-raised child for the most part. And then, before I started my junior year of high school, I came out to Colorado to help my mom take care of her parents for a little while so I could also take college classes…it was a final chance to experience something different before real adult life kicks in."

"Are you excited to jump into Pink Every Day with the girls after graduation? I know you've been doing some behind-the-scenes stuff, but Matt was saying that you'd be joining the team fully after graduation."

"That's the plan. I'm ready for it. Not sure what my mom is going to be doing yet. She mentioned she wouldn't mind staying out here with me, but Dad is also getting antsy about having us back home. He doesn't see the work I do with Sasha as being 'legit', so he's made some comments about needing to find an actual job once I'm done playing with makeup." Jonathan shakes his head, and I can't believe I just unloaded all of that. Sasha and Ashley don't even know all that I just shared with him.

"He must not know you very well, then, because the work you are all doing with the company is so much more than makeup. Even I know that. Hopefully, he sees some of the newest campaigns this fall and can see the good you're doing to help other businesses and initiatives."

"A girl can hope."

13

• June

• Wednesday

2:00 tail light replacement

165 201

• Week 24

04 46 21 10
01 15 24

July
26 27 28 29 30 31
01 02 03 04 05 06 07
08 09 10 11 12 13 14
15 16 17 18 19 20 21
22 23 24 25 26 27 28

Chapter Seven

JONATHAN

PEANUT BUTTER BANANA PROTEIN SMOOTHIE

Social Post: What's in your travel auto kit? I've been looking at updating mine, but here's what I have for when I need to fly. #travelkit #masterscarrestoration #classiccars #autokit

Image Description: Photo of my travel auto kit with the very few items that actually are approved to fly with. I'll probably need to stop and pick up a few things once we land in Montana.

I don't have to travel often to pick up cars. And when I do, I usually do it by myself. I'm not 100 percent sure why I thought it important to have someone with me this time. Maybe I was just trying to find a reason to spend more time with Tilly. She's been hanging around the friend group for the last four years now. And she fits in so well with the rest of the girls. Sometimes she can be a little reserved, and other times she gets so excited about things that she doesn't realize she's been talking for

five minutes without taking a breath. A little exaggeration there, but not much.

I can tell she's been told a lot that she takes up too much space or isn't doing what she should be doing. She questions herself a lot. Not always out loud. It's actually usually done in her head, but I can see the indecision and doubt after she says what she wants. She worries over how she's perceived.

And if I have one goal in mind for the next day and a half outside of getting this car back home safe – it's taking every opportunity to show this incredible woman just how much she doesn't have to do that around me.

The drive back to Colorado isn't terribly long when able to drive straight through, but this car is not in the best shape, so I planned to split it up between two days to make sure I could take my time and not damage the engine or any other parts more than they already are. But as I look over the car before I take possession of it, it's in worse shape than I was when I talked to the shop owner last week.

"You told me over the phone that all this work was already completed, and all I needed to do was a few internal tune-ups and then the external body work. I'm not going to be able to take this thing over forty on the highway with how it sounds, just running in the parking lot." I try to stay professional and calm with how I talk to the shop owner. But this is less than ideal. Especially because I have Tilly with me, and I didn't tell her there was a possibility of this trip extending further than tomorrow night. But if I push this car more than that, it's going to be destroyed. And I don't have the time or money for that right now.

"I'm sorry if that's what you thought you heard, but this is what it is. The car owner signed off on it, and I need it off my lot. Here's your paperwork," he says as he hands it over, crinkled and coffee-stained. I cringe internally, wondering what else I'm going to find in this car once I get it back to my shop. "There are snacks and water inside if you and your girl want to grab anything before you go." He motions toward the reception area, and I pull the keys from the ignition before following him inside.

'My girl' – I like the sound of that.

It takes my eyes a minute to adjust to the inside of the building. It smells like grease and stale coffee in here. Not at all the welcoming space that you want to go over quotes and designs with a potential buyer or a car collector. But I guess this guy is only doing quick flips and generic sales. Hence, why I'm picking up this one for Mason. Tilly is over by one of the walls, looking at photos of classic cars. Her hair is up in a messy bun, and the tiredness is visible in her eyes even from here. But I don't miss the way her eyes light up when she recognizes one of the cars.

"This is the one you are working on at the shop, isn't it?" She's pointing to a two-door Chevrolet Corvette. It's not the right year, but at least she recognized the style and model. I nod and walk over to the wall. There are a lot of nice cars here. I take a moment to take them all in before pointing out another one.

"This is what we're picking up today, and then this is one I get to start working on soon for a client in Chicago." It's not hard to spot the Charger that's sitting outside now, and then the Shelby that I'll get to spend the next several weeks bringing back into original condition.

"Chicago? I didn't realize restoring cars would have you traveling so much. Is this usually how it is for you?" She seems almost a little uneasy with that question, and I wonder what she's worried about.

"It depends on the jobs and how things are going that season. Some years I haven't traveled at all, and others I'm doing things like this trip with flying to go pick up vehicles and then shipping others off to buyers after I get the restorations finished. I don't know if I need to be the one to deliver the Chicago car yet or not. I'll find that out once we get a little closer to completion on that one. Don't worry," I add to try to get that smile back on her face that was there most of the morning, "I won't ask you to come with me every time. I know you have work you need to do for school and your social media obligations with Sasha."

"Oh, I don't mind. I think this might be kind of fun. And I like that you thought of me for this. It gives me a chance to travel and see parts of the country that I might not have the chance to otherwise. And maybe I'll even learn something." The hopeful look in her eyes as she gazes up at me nearly makes me reach for her hand to reassure her that I do like having her here. She only comes up to mid-chest height on me, and I love the way she looks up at me when she's talking.

Instead, I rest my hand on her arm, just above her elbow, for just a beat or two before letting my hand fall away. "I like having you here with me, too. This may take us a bit longer than I initially planned, but I'll get you back to Fort Collins as soon as I can. Safely, that is."

"Sounds good," her shy smile brings a similar one to my face. This girl is just too cute, and I don't miss the way her cheeks pinked when I touched her a moment ago. "So, are we ready to go?"

"After you, Tilly," I hold the door open for her, and we are on our way.

The first few hours of the trip aren't bad. It was early morning when we left the shop in Montana, and it's only now approaching noon. As it gets warmer, I start worrying more about the state of this car. The temperature gauge on the dash keeps spiking up and then taking its sweet time coming back down. We are fifteen minutes away from the next town, so I'm crossing my fingers, toes, and everything else, hoping we can at least make it there. I'm going to need more coolant and a bunch of water before we try to go any further.

"Is it supposed to be doing that?" Tilly's voice pulls me out of my worrying, and I immediately notice the light steam coming out of the hood of the car.

"No, it's not." I know my answer came out a little clipped, but I cannot afford for this car to give out on me here. I need to get to town so I can actually see what needs to be fixed. Reluctantly, I pull over to the side of the highway, hit the button for the hazard lights, and then roll down the windows.

"This isn't going to be fun, and I apologize in advance." That's all the warning I give her before I blast the heat as high as it will go.

Tilly's giggle is not what I expected her to respond with, but it helps ease the tension I'm feeling over this car right now. "Is it not hot enough? You need to make it hotter?"

"Running the heat internally like this helps pull some of the heat off the engine block. I think the last shop stretched the truth a bit on the work they did, so the engine is running hot. I need to cool it down enough to get us to town, where I'll be able to get some more coolant and extra water. And hopefully, I can tweak a few little things so we can get home in a decent amount of time."

"Do we need to stay in town before trying again tomorrow? I know this car is for one of your best customers...or is it clients? How *do* you refer to the guys you work with?" I smile at her question – the desire to learn more about what I do at every opportunity.

"'Buyer' if I don't really have an established relationship with them. Other than that, it's 'collector' or 'client' usually. And yes, this is one of Mason's cars. I've worked on most of the cars in his collection. Unfortunately, he's in Europe right now, so I'm limited on when I can speak with him. And that's probably why the other shop tried to pull the things they did on this project." I shake my head as I watch the engine's temperature slowly fall closer to where I need it to be. Turning off the car, I pop the lock on the hood before grabbing my few tools I could fly with out of the trunk.

Tilly gets out of the car, too, and walks around to watch me work. And even though I'm sure she has no idea what I'm doing over here, she doesn't ask me a bunch of questions. She just takes it all in and is there to hold my flashlight or wrench as I pass them to her. Within a few minutes, I at least know what the problem is.

"Let's see how she's doing now. Hopefully, we can get to town without any further problems, and then we can reassess from there. Are you okay if this ends up taking another day?"

"Whatever you need, Jonathan. I'm all yours."

Chapter Eight

TILLY

ROSE CARDAMOM TEA LATTE

Social Post: How cute is this coffee shop? I stopped in real quick while we had to make a stop on our drive back to Colorado today. And they had this super fun tea latte that I just had to try. Have you had something with this flavor combination before? #localtea #localcoffee #localfinds #rosecardamom #tealattes

Image Description: My drink on the counter of the coffee house.

Ooooh, that came out so much flirtier than I intended. Do you think he noticed? Yeah, he probably did, considering the way his smirk grew and my cheeks heated as soon as I said it. I'm constantly tripping over my words (and myself) around this man. He's tall and in great shape and absolutely gorgeous. And he works with his hands. I don't know why, but I kind of love that he doesn't have an office job. He gets dirty and has muscles that have been built by working on cars and helping Luca with his own woodworking and furniture projects – not in a gym. Not that gym muscles are bad. Or office jobs. But I like that he works hard. It shows.

I don't miss the little chuckle that Jonathan gives at my last statement, and I pretend not to notice. 'Pretend' being the key word there. I send up a silent prayer that I can tone back the awkwardness and that we make it to town without any further car scares. I won't be upset about an extra day on the road if that's what we end up having to do, though. These few days away from school, preparing social media campaigns – and pretending that I'm not getting closer to the day when my father insists I come home – are needed. And the longer I'm sitting in this car with Jonathan, the more I realize that.

"I think this is our exit up here," I point out when I see the sign for the town. Smiling when I see that there are several options for shopping, food, and lodging. So, if we do end up stranded here for the rest of the day, we'll have some things to choose from.

Jonathan doesn't say anything, but he signals over and begins preparing to take the exit ramp. As if the car can sense the upcoming break, the car starts blinking that temperature gauge again. Yes, I had actually been paying attention when he was pointing out what he was worried about before. Don't ask me to explain all the semantics, but I know the little arm isn't supposed to be that close to the 'H' on the dial. I lean over to turn on the heat and roll down my window, hoping it's enough to stave off another unplanned stop before we get to the auto parts store.

"One more mile, come on," I hear Jonathan mutter under his breath. He's not angry, though. It's an encouragement. Car guys do refer to their cars as 'girls' so I guess it fits that he's talking to it, her. I'll get all the terminology figured out eventually.

I'm sure I'll start understanding it as soon as it's time for me to go back home. Because inevitably, Mayor Chance is going to make me come back to 'real life' eventually. I don't want to go back to Chicago. I don't want a job in a stuffy office or playing the part of a politician's wife. I like my life here. My friends, my found family, my classes, and the work I get to do alongside that group are so much more than just makeup and social media. We're doing actual work to help women business owners get the resources they need to grow. We are helping Colorado cosmetic brands be more sustainable and user-friendly. And we're giving back to women-owned organizations with every campaign we are able to complete. If I am given a say in what my future will hold, it's going to be more of this. This is where I am at my happiest.

I don't even realize we've parked, with being so consumed with my own internal discussion. Jonathan opening my door and bending a little to make eye contact with me nearly makes me jump, which is when I notice we're outside of the auto parts store, and the hood is popped on the car again.

"Sorry, I was totally in my own little world there for a minute." I am doing that a lot around him. I don't think it's him though, there's just way too much going on in my head right now. I grab my purse and get out of the car, trying to subtly peel the fabric of my shirt away from my sweaty back as I do. Gross.

"No worries, Tilly. I have to go inside to get a few things and then work on this for a bit. I know you brought some things to do and I don't know how long I'll need to be here. Do you want to walk over to the coffee shop over there and get your stuff done?" He points at the cute coffee shop slash bakery across the parking lot with the cutest panda and cherry blossom logo. It's actually quite adorable.

"Do you not want me to help or hold a flashlight or keep you company? I'm sorry if I was in the way earlier."

"You're not in the way, Tilly. I like having you here, helping or chatting, or even just being with me. But I know you have other obligations too, and I can guarantee Wi-Fi now, while I have to get up close and personal with little Miss Charger over here."

"Charger isn't a very pretty name for a beautiful girl like this one." I can't believe how flirty I'm being right now.

Jonathan's laugh is rich, and he smiles with his whole face. I like that. "Do you want to name Mason's newest lady?"

"I'll have to think on that. But I'll let you know. But seriously, I'm happy to hang out with you out here. I have some time before the next campaign is due, and I don't have any school assignments yet."

"Okay then, let's go explore the store together." He holds his arm out like he's escorting me inside, and I do a mock curtsey before I walk next to him.

So, maybe I zoned out while in the store. The packaging wasn't pretty, and nothing had easy-to-recognize terms or uses. Maybe these brands could learn something from beauty and skincare packaging. Sure, all the light bulbs were together, but why on earth are there so many? And there's a universal good, better, and best system that people just seem to know when looking at them. Why bother with the good level at all, then? And don't even get me started on the windshield wipers. You have to look it up in a book to figure out what you need. Every time. Unless you happen to remember which letter and number combination belongs to your car. Why don't they make them universal?

"I think I figured out her name," I tell Jonathan as we finally go back outside, and I can get a full breath of fresh air again.

"Whose name?" He pops the hood again and refills the coolant before playing around with other knobs and things.

"The car. I told you she needed a name."

"So, what's her name?" Jonathan chuckles his response back at me.

"Val."

"Like Valerie or what?"

"Valentine."

"Why Valentine?"

"Because she's a pretty red color."

"I feel like there's more to that answer than you're giving me."

"Okay, don't judge me – but it's the name of the FMC in my favorite Mafia romance book."

You know that funny moment in movies where the girl says something ridiculous and the guy bangs his head on the hood of the car because he's trying to make eye contact too quickly to make sure he heard that right? Yeah…it happens in real life too. And we just had that moment. I squeal when he hits his head and run over to make sure he's okay.

"I'm good, I just – what did you say?" The smile on his face brightens his eyes, even though it's still obvious how tired and stressed he is right now. At first glance, I thought they were brown, but he has green flecks in them too. They're probably a hazel color if I had to classify them as a specific shade.

"So, when I'm not doing makeup and skincare stuff or in class, I really enjoy reading. Mostly romance novels, but a little bit of everything. And my favorite author focuses on plus-size FMCs – that's female main characters – and I like being able to see a bit of myself in those stories. Seeing that girls who look like me are just as deserving of love and romance."

"And the Mafia thing?"

"Oh, yeah, she has a Mafia series. So basically, all the guys in the series are morally grey. Doing everything to take care of their girls and show them they love them and would do anything for them. But have zero problem unaliving other people if they threaten their happiness. It's totally a red flag, but in romance novels, it's the best."

"Okay then, I'll text Mason and let him know that his new car is now Valentine, or he can call her Val if that fits better." I'm not sure if he's just coddling me, but it seems like he's okay with all the word vomit I just threw at him. And I'm going to believe that in this moment that I'm not annoying him or taking up too much space. He asked a question. I answered it. And I'm allowed to do just that.

"Perfect. Now, what else does Miss Val need before we decide on next steps?"

The next hour consists of Jonathan working on Valentine, with me trying to listen to his explanations. I know I'm not going to retain all of it. But I enjoy listening. And I made myself comfortable on a bench outside the auto shop to get some emails answered for Sasha and Pink Every Day while we waited for some sort of fluid to cycle through the engine while it ran for a bit. Don't ask me what fluid, though, because I have no idea. We are getting ready for our big October campaigns, so it's time for final approvals, that way we are fully ready to go before October first.

Pink Every Day was Sasha's social media baby a few years ago. It started as just a campaign she ran with a local woman-owned business as a way to highlight them and other woman-owned brands throughout the month. That campaign was what brought her in front of a lot of major industry names. And it quickly grew into a full business. In the first year, she was able to bring Ashley on board, only part-time, since she was still in college. Ashley handles product development, and that girl knows her stuff. That's when the company went from supporting local initiatives and woman-owned brands to actually creating products.

Now, Pink Every Day has ten full-time employees, an actual office building, and a small warehouse. Hopefully, we'll have a storefront within the next three years. I get to handle social media for Sasha and Pink Every Day now that she deals with more of the official CEO stuff, like the boss babe she is. And she has offered me the Head of Marketing title once I graduate. And I so badly want to say 'yes,' I'm just incredibly scared that my dad is going to come in and rip it all away just as I get myself established into something I love.

But I decided when I moved out here that I'm going to give this my everything. For however long I'm going to have it. My job, my hobbies, my schoolwork, and my friends. I'm going to own my joy today. Because he can't take that away from me.

13

• June

• Wednesday

2:00 tail light replacement

185-201

• Week - 24

Chapter Nine

JONATHAN

ROSE BLACK TEA LATTE

Social Post: Apparently, we are drinking rose themed drinks on this trip. And because this is the account for Masters Car Restoration, here's the results of our pit stop. It's been a long day, but we are ready to call it a night and head the rest of the way back tomorrow. #masterscarrestoration #tealattes #rosedrinks #autobodywork #roadtripping

Image Description: Empty packs of supplies from the auto parts store along with two pink tea lattes. They're actually really good. Don't judge.

Tilly may be totally clueless when it comes to cars, but having her here with me while I work has made today spectacular. Granted, I wanted to be a whole lot farther in our trip by now, not three hours from where we started. But I've gotten to know Miss Val a lot better already, and Tilly as well. When given the chance, that girl can talk. And I love hearing her voice, her words, her passions. And even her doubts. Those don't

come through as clearly, but I'm a good listener. And with her, I'm hanging on every word like it's the most important thing I'll hear today.

"So, when are we going to try to keep going with the drive? Do you want to get a couple of hours in now it's starting to cool down, or do you want to try to find someplace close by to spend the night? I'm up for whatever, but want to see what you are thinking," Her question is tentative, like she doesn't want to upset me, but I can see the fatigue in her eyes and the way she holds her body while standing. She's been up just as long as I have, and it's been a long day.

"Let's call it a night here. I'd feel better hitting the road again in the morning and trying to go until around one or two, or whenever Miss Val decides that she is done for the day. I at least know we can get a nicer and cleaner place here than other places we may have to stop if we continue today. That good with you?" I drop the hood and go around the car to set my tools and the items I picked up at the store back into the trunk.

"Yep, sounds good. I've already found an available room in one of the hotels in town. It has two queen beds. I wasn't sure what the budget was since it looks like we may have an additional hotel stay, but figured we could be mature and share a room. I probably shouldn't have assumed, but I reserved it. We can cancel it if needed, but I didn't want us to be without options if you wanted to wait a little longer." Her rambling is cute. I walk closer to her and put my hand over her phone, which she is still scrolling through, probably seeing if she can find a better deal for a hotel.

"Whatever you booked is great, Tilly. Thank you." My voice is steady and appreciative, and I smile gently when she looks up at me. Hopefully, she isn't mad that I interrupted her or stopped her from what she was doing.

When her eyes meet mine, there is a settled vibe I get from her, like she is almost surprised that I don't have any objections to what she did.

"I'm glad it's one less thing that I need to think about. Do you want to go grab takeout, or do you want to go sit and eat somewhere?" I try changing the subject a bit, focusing on something

56

that I can control, like feeding her. She's here to help me, and I have no problem making sure she's taken care of in exchange for that.

"Are you all right if I say takeout? I'm all sweaty and gross and don't want to be out in public long enough to eat a meal. I'd be way too self-conscious." Her fingers toy with the hem of her shirt as she says it, and I notice her pulling the fabric away from her back, the slight wetness of her hair along her forehead. I shouldn't have let her be out in the sun all day. Has she had enough to drink? Is she getting heat stroke? How do you know if someone is exhibiting symptoms?

"Of course. I'm so sorry I didn't think of having you in the shade longer. Are you feeling okay? Let's pack up and grab some food, and then head to the hotel. We'll call it a night so we can be on the road first thing."

"Yeah, I'm okay. Just desperately needing a shower and to lie down for a little while. And maybe some ice cream if we can find it on the way."

"Done."

The laughter Tilly lets out when she opens the hotel door is incredible. She opens it while holding our drinks and ice cream, and I have all the rest of our stuff. The things we do to avoid making a second trip to the car.

"What's so funny? Please tell me this is a normal hotel room and not a sex room." I try to peek around her, but don't see any glaring red flags. I do, however, only see one bed.

"It's a normal room, we are just checking off all the cliché romance novel tropes on this trip. The car that breaks down, only one bed..." She trails off as she sets the drinks on the small desk in the corner.

"I can call down and see if they have any double bed rooms still available. I promise I booked a double earlier," she mumbles as she pulls out her phone again.

"Tilly, it's okay. I don't mind if you don't. We're both adults. We're both exhausted and just need a clean and quiet place to rest before we start again tomorrow. Let's eat and try to get some sleep. I'd like to be on the road at five tomorrow if that's okay with you. I don't know how long we'll be able to go before Miss Val needs another break."

"Are you sure?" Her question is hopeful, and I know she needs to hear I'm not upset. I have to force myself not to walk over and give her a hug, but I know she mentioned she was sweaty and uncomfortable. I don't need to give her additional things to worry about.

"I'm positive, Tilly. This is great. It's a nice hotel and exactly what we need. Please don't stress about this. I appreciate you and all you are doing on this little excursion."

"Even naming your client's car?"

"Even that."

TILLY

I took my sweet time in the shower once we finished eating. I needed the time to work through my thoughts, my emotions, and try to get a handle on my desire to voice every thought that comes into my head. Of course, the hotel only has one bed. Why did I think the universe would have anything else in store for us on this trip? At least the hotel has good shampoo and conditioner in here – the kind that I can use to shave my legs since I neglected to bring any shaving cream, just my razor. And I only brought a nightshirt to wear and not full pajamas. Because again, why on earth would I think we would be sharing a room, much less a bed? *Yay me.*

Once I finish in the shower and am properly skin prepped, moisturized, and hair brushed, oiled, and dried, I take a deep breath and open the door to the bedroom. Only to see a half-naked

Jonathan pulling down the sheets on the bed. Our eyes don't meet. Not right away, anyway. His eyes land on my bare legs just as I take in his toned chest, his solid arms, and the trail of hair that goes from his belly button to below his waistband. Oh, this is a very, very bad idea.

13

• June

• Wednesday

2:00 tail light replacement

185-201

• Week · 24

☀ 04:46 ☾ 21:10
☽ 01:15 **24**

• July

Chapter Ten

JONATHAN

CHAMOMILE LAVENDER TEA

Social Post: Anyone else getting excited over the new models this year? While I definitely prefer working on classic cars, I'm liking the trends that are coming out recently. #newcars #carrestoration #autobodywork #coloradocardealers

Image Description: Slide show of new models from Chevrolet, Ford, and Lexus.

While Tilly is in the shower, I go through emails and a few waiting invoices for projects in the garage back home. This is the part of the job I don't necessarily love, but it's a requirement. Maybe one day, I'll be able to fully pass this on to someone else. But for now, it helps me stay on top of every project, every dollar, and know where we are in the process for each rebuild or smaller touch-up. I also map out where I hope to be by tomorrow night and tentatively book a room in a hotel in town. I don't want to end up stranded and not have a space to stay. Crossing my fingers that Miss Val behaves and we get where we want to go without any more unplanned detours.

"Mafia romance..." I never would have thought that Tilly would be the one to bring that up, but now, I'm definitely intrigued.

I love that I get to spend time with the gorgeous girl I have the opportunity to share a room with tonight. But she has to get ready for classes, and I don't want to push my luck with making this road trip longer than absolutely necessary. Hopefully, we'll have other opportunities to spend time together after we get back home. After taking care of all the admin stuff, I start preparing for bed. As much as I can before I am able to shower, that is. I'm normally a morning shower guy, but after the travel and work I had today, I need to freshen up before I'll be able to comfortably rest tonight. I should probably make sure the sheets are okay before we get too settled in. And just as I'm pulling back the blanket to check, the door opens to the bathroom and I see the most gorgeous pair of legs I've ever laid my eyes on.

I don't miss the blush that immediately rushes over her cheeks and spreads down her neck. I clear my throat and force my eyes away from the incredible woman in front of me.

"I was just making sure the sheets are all good so we don't have to call down for new ones before it gets too late. How was the shower?" *How was the shower?* Who talks like that?

"It was good. Good pressure, and it stayed hot the whole time, so I might have spent a bit too long in there," she chuckles her response before putting her things back in her bag. I don't miss the shine on her legs or the way her hair smells as she passes. I know it's not her normal scent, but it still entices me. Hands to yourself, Jonathan.

"Good to hear. I'm going to take a quick shower and then try to get some sleep. Outlets are on both sides of the bed, so pick which side you want. I have my alarm set for four-thirty, so I should be ready to go by five. Not sure how long you'll need in the morning, but if you need me to adjust, let me know." I pick up my clothes and start heading to the bathroom, desperately needing some space while she gets settled. I can't be trusted being that close to her naked legs. Because all I can think about is what color her thighs would be under my touch – would they pink up or go whiter before leaving behind the evidence that my hands have been on her? Nope, not going there.

"That should be fine. I'll just need to get dressed and freshen up a bit. I do most of my in-depth skin and hair care at night so I don't have to spend a lot of time getting ready in the morning. Oh, I probably should have asked. Did you need any skin or hair stuff? I'm not sure if you packed light because of the plane ride or what you normally bring. If you use that stuff, that is, not that I care either way. I just want to offer, just in case. You probably don't use any of this. I'll just put it away." Her jabbering keeps going as she shuffles around in her bag, and I just smile at her rambling.

"I actually do follow a full skincare routine. Sasha got Matt some stuff last year and then gave it to Luca and me as well. She might have gotten some stuff for Marcus, too. I'm not sure. There was some light convincing, but we all decided to give it a try. Anyway, I take care of my skin. And yes, it's more than just a bar of soap." Her smile at that comment brings another one to my face. "I don't do much with my hair, but I did bring my skincare with me. Thanks for offering, though. Try to get some rest and quiet. Four-thirty comes early."

I don't allow myself a full breath until the bathroom door closes between us. Tonight might be a lot harder than I thought. But I'm an adult and can keep my hands to myself. She's here as my friend, and I can respect that.

By the time I finish in the shower, I hear her voice on the other side of the door. She must be on the phone, but she doesn't sound happy with whoever she's talking to. I quickly get dressed and towel dry my hair. I don't think I've ever gotten ready for bed so quickly, but I want to know what's going on. I'm quiet as I make my way into the room. Tilly makes eye contact, acknowledging my presence, but staying focused on her conversation.

"But, I'm about to start my last year of classes. I'm so close to being done. And I have my job lined up for afterward. This is what I want, Dad. Why are you still pushing this?" I keep my eyes away from hers, but I'm not leaving this room. I can hear the voice on the other end, and it isn't happy. Although I can't understand his words, he has to have his voice raised at her, with how well I can hear him from across the room.

"I told you, I don't want to be a perfect little politician's wife. I don't know why you keep talking to Jason's dad as if this is already a done deal. I broke up with him when I was sixteen, right before I came out here with Mom. I haven't talked to him or heard from him since." She's quiet for another moment, and I come sit on the other side of the bed, scrolling on my phone without actually seeing anything. I needed to be closer to her.

"What do you mean you kept the signed contract? Who does that? I thought it was something you had talked about keeping, but that when I called things off with Jason and then moved out here that you nullified it. I have my plan for my future in the works, and having a husband that you picked out for me isn't part of that agenda."

Another break in conversation, and I chance a look. The tears in the corners of her eyes break my heart a little, and I wish I could take away her sadness.

"I need you to get out of it. Destroy it, write up another one that cancels out the first, tell Jason that I moved to Fiji and you can't find me. This isn't happening." If it were fifteen years prior, she would have slammed the phone down on the receiver, but she settles for hitting the end button and then powering off her phone.

"That sounded fun," I offer, trying to give her a chance to talk if she wants it, but also giving her the space to direct the conversation.

"Not really. You'd think my dad was actually royalty with the way he handles business and professional relationships. I knew he wanted me to get with a business friend's son, and neither of our dads was happy when we broke up. But we were sixteen. It wasn't actually going anywhere."

"So why is he bringing it up again now?"

"The dads decided to sign a contract that Jason, my high school boyfriend, and I would get married so Jason could take over the business seat and have a stable wife at home waiting for him. Showing off the American ideal of a couple in power or something like that. He had said something about a contract when I was still living at home, but I honestly thought it was gotten rid of once Mom and I moved out here."

"Wow, that's crazy." I allow myself a second to take in her response before I try to push a bit further, "What are the ramifications of getting out of the contract? That can't be fully legal, can it?"

"Honestly? I don't know, Jonathan. I just want to stay in this little bubble a little longer without worrying about anything." She takes a deep breath and then gets settled into the covers. "Good night, Jonathan. I'll see you in the morning."

"Good night, Tilly."

I don't fall asleep until after one. I know it's going to come back to bite me in the morning, but I have so many questions. Who's Tilly's dad? Why is he doing this to her? How much longer can she continue to pretend he isn't making these demands? And how can I help her take back her own agency? Because, I think that's what I need to do. It's definitely what I want to do. If she'll let me.

Chapter Eleven

TILLY

SMOOTHIE KING ANGEL FOOD

Social Post: Lipstick makes everything better. #lippie #dailylippie #completelytilly

Image Description: Product flat lay with a sugar scrub, lip liner, and lipstick along with the hotel notebook and pen from where we stayed last night.

Who on earth, in the time of TikTok, Taylor Swift, and transfer-proof lip stain, decides to sign an actual marriage contract for their fully adult daughter to a business partner's equally adult son without their consent? Are you kidding me right now? I've been awake for fifteen minutes, staring at the ceiling, asking myself this exact series of questions over and over again. I haven't spoken to Jason in literally five years. I don't even remember his parents' first names. Did he go to college? What does he want to do with his life? Is he still a total finance bro that thinks his wife needs to be a size four, platinum-blonde, who goes to Pilates and brunch every morning with a bunch of copy/paste beauty queens? Nothing against those girls, that's just not me.

I'm a size sixteen on a good day. More recently, I've been comfortable in a size eighteen. I'm curvy all over. I have stretch marks and a squishy belly. My breasts aren't even in size or shape, and they completely fill my DD cups. My hair isn't dyed. I like my natural brown hair that sometimes curls, sometimes frizzes, and is usually doing its own thing. I find comfort in knowing that my body takes care of me. I own my size and love dressing up in it. Plus-size fashion has come a long way, and I love wearing sparkly dresses, high heels, and jeans that show off my curves. I love wearing bright colors, bold lipstick, and matching my shoes with my handbag. Yes, I am that girl.

But, I also love learning about marketing trends, makeup products, and skincare that leads to sustainable production and jobs for moms who need them. I get to be an active part in making that happen with my job at Pink Every Day. And I don't want to give that up just to have a title of "wife" without any of the responsibility of what I'm doing now. I don't let the tears fall. Who does he think he is? This is not happening.

I finally sit up and turn my phone back on. I don't even bother opening any of the messages from my dad. I just texted my mom to let her know what happened and that I'm hoping to be home sometime early tomorrow.

> Mom: I'll talk to him. This shouldn't have happened without your consent or at least a conversation with me and you. I'll let you know what I find out. I, too, was under the assumption that this wasn't ever official and if it was, it was done away with when we moved to Colorado.

Me: Thank you. Keep me updated. I may be out of cell signal for a bit today as we drive, but I'll check in when I can.

Mom: Sounds good. Be safe. Use protection.

Me: <face palm emoji>

Mom: Love you

Me: Love you too.

Time to get ready for another day.

We are six hours into our drive when Miss Val decides she is done for the day. At least we've made some progress. I think we're only five hours from home, so we should be back early tomorrow. Jonathan took care of hotel reservations this time around. And I'm thankful that I didn't have to worry about it. Not that I minded finding the space yesterday, I could tell he was stressed over all the things happening. And it was something I could control, something I could help with. I can listen to him chatting about engines, oils, and gauges all day long, even if I still won't be able to do more than hold the flashlight and admire the way his butt looks in his jeans while he bends over the engine. What? Have you seen this man's ass? It's that good, I promise.

"The hotel doesn't start early check-in until one, so we have a little bit of time. Drive-thru or lunch at a place today?" Jonathan asks as he pulls out of the gas station and heads toward the hotel we will be staying at tonight. This town is super cute. Don't ask me where we are, because again, I don't know. But it gives classic

Americana vibes. I think there may be five stoplights in the whole thing. A Wal-Mart, a coffee shop, a thrift store, an antique store, a candy place, and a couple of restaurants line the main street. I think we are on the outskirts of a busier city, because there shouldn't need to be two hotels here. But it's cozy.

"I think lunch sounds good. It'll give Val a chance to cool in the shade, and we can have an actual meal while she naps." I pull up a travel app on my phone to see what might be a good option in town for lunch while Jonathan chuckles beside me. "What's so funny?"

"You're just adorable, do you know that?"

"I try." I give him a smirk and keep scrolling until I find a family-owned restaurant that gets good reviews. I point it out, and Jonathan finds a parking spot in the shade. I get out of the car while he blasts the heat again, trying to get her down to a manageable temperature. When he deems she is ready for her nap, we head inside.

While I knew this was a family-owned place, I didn't realize they were a very traditional, very excited Greek family. The restaurant is filled with subtle whites and blues that bring a sense of peace and desire to be by the water. The music playing is an instrumental mix that sounds like popular covers, but has some folk music and other songs I don't recognize mixed in. We are greeted by the cutest grandmother ever, and I'm pretty sure she has to remind herself she isn't allowed to kiss the cheeks of the guests before showing us to a booth in the corner. There are only about ten tables in here, plus the seating at the bar. I think this place can only comfortably seat forty-five, maybe fifty people.

I take my time looking over the menu, and Jonathan does the same. I haven't had Greek food in a while. We order with the same grandmother and then a guy around our age comes out with iced tea and water for both of us. He also brings out our tzatziki appetizer, and I don't hesitate to dig in. I love this stuff!

"Have you ever had this before?" I ask Jonathan as I dip another piece of pita bread in the lemon and dill, yogurt dip.

"I don't think so. I wasn't able to have a lot of creativity in food choices when I was younger, and I tend to stick with comfort foods now. It's just me at home most of the time, except when I have my sister's boys. I cook when they come over, but I do most of my experimenting with smoothies and juices since it's a little easier to grab and go on busier days. What about you?"

At least he isn't shy about trying new things, and I think he likes it. He dips a carrot in the dip and then uses his tongue to clean up a bit of it left on the outside of his lip. Okay, not looking at that. Talk. He asked me a question.

"Um, yeah. I guess there were some benefits to growing up in a politician's house. There were lots of dinners and luncheons at the Country Club. I've tried a lot of ethnic foods, and then there wasn't a lot of opportunity to not like something. Even if it wasn't my favorite, I had to take bites and eat what I was given. It doesn't exactly look good to turn down a meal from the President, ya know?" Jonathan just levels his eyes at me. "What? Do I have tzatziki on my face?" I dab at my lips with a napkin and wait for him to find his words again.

"No, you're fine. You just said that like it was any other Tuesday, and not having a meal with the actual President of the country. That's pretty cool. How old were you?" I smirk before answering.

"Which time?"

When we get to our hotel and to our room, I'm ready for a nap. Even though I went with a lighter meal, I am exhausted. But I'm not lucky enough to be able to lay down right away. My phone rings as soon as I drop my bag on my bed. Yes, my bed. There are two in this one.

"Hey, Mom, we just got to our hotel. What's up?"

"Hey, Tilly. I spoke with your dad and then our lawyer and then your dad again about the whole contract that he signed with Jason's dad."

"That's a lot of phone calls. What did you find out?" I sit on the edge of the bed. Part of me wants to take out a notebook so I

The Ride For You

can write things down and have it all laid out in front of me, but I know I don't have the mental capacity for all that right now.

"Well, it's legally binding. It's notarized and done up properly. I don't know why I wasn't consulted on it, or you weren't at least made aware it was being talked about. You and Jason are to be married before your twenty-second birthday. Once you've been married for five years, Jason will inherit your shares of your father's company. The one that he has been working on while holding the mayor's seat."

"Wait, what company? I didn't know Dad was doing anything..." My voice trails off. How many secrets has this man been holding onto while we were in Colorado?

"I wasn't aware of it either. Apparently, he has been investing in a few different ventures and has grown to be the majority shareholder in four companies. I'm not sure how legal it is since he is in a position of government, but none of the companies reside in the state where he does, so I think that's the workaround."

"Great, so which one is Jason going to get as a wedding present?"

"That's the not-fun part and the piece that I had to spend a little time digging into. Because I thought it sounded familiar when he mentioned it."

"Which one, Mom?" My heart drops as I wait for her response.

"The supplier Pink Every Day just signed a five-year contract with."

"You have got to be joking, what happens if I don't marry Jason and let him take over this company in five years?" I don't even want to hear her answer, but I need to know what the alternative is. There has to be a way to save everything that I've been building. I can feel Jonathan on the other side of the room. He's listening and taking it all in, but not interrupting until I let him know it's okay. His presence is more comforting than I expected, but it is so needed.

"Then the company dissolves. Your father did some research, Tilly. If this doesn't happen, Pink Every Day won't have the resources they need to continue." I blow out a breath and will the tears to stay put.

"If I'm understanding this right, we have five years to get

72

something else figured out? That's not that bad. We can work with that." I think I'm convincing myself more than anything right now.

"No, Tilly." Mom takes a deep breath and then continues. "The supplier is set to renegotiate contracts the day after your twenty-second birthday. If you aren't married to Jason by that time, your father is going to dissolve the company. And he's well within his rights to. If you don't go along with the contract, Pink Every Day will very likely not be around a year from today. They won't have product, they won't have the resources that were promised, and they won't be able to fulfill the contracts they have signed for the next year. The collaborations will fail because Pink Every Day can't hold on to their end. There won't be a way to salvage it, Tilly."

"I have to marry Jason before January. And stay married to him for at least five years?" I hate the words even as I say them.

"Yes, love. That's the basics of it. There's a lot more to it, and my lawyer is looking over the contract now to see if there is any other loophole we can work through. But your dad isn't playing around. He did his research, and he's going after what you care most about."

"Okay, I'll chat with you soon. Keep me updated."

"I will. I love you. We'll figure this out. Jason is going to call you at some point this week to connect and set up a time to come visit you. I'm going to leave that fully up to you because you're an adult and you get to set the rules for that."

"Okay. I'll be watching for it, I guess. I'm going to need to go and lie down for a bit. I think we can start chatting wedding plans when I get home tomorrow."

"I love you. We'll figure it out."

"Love you too, Mom."

I don't even look before I toss my phone on the ground and then fall backward on the bed. I let the tears fall as I let every single emotion play out in my thoughts. All the what-ifs, the possibilities, the jobs that will be lost, the collaborations that will be canceled. My job is going to be gone. I either won't have the life I've been building for myself, or there will be at least fifteen people who will lose their happiness and dreams. Plus, over three hundred thousand dollars' worth of contracts that we are set to fulfill within the next thirty-six months.

"What do you need, pretty girl?" I open my eyes and see Jonathan staring. I didn't even feel him crawl onto the bed beside me, but he doesn't ask questions or demand an explanation. He doesn't tell me to stop crying or start calling people to fix stuff. He puts it back in my hands.

"I know it sounds really weird, but can you just hold me for a little bit?"

"I would be honored, come here." And with that, he opens his arms and lets me snuggle in close. And I let the tears fall, soaking his shirt as he soothes me with his hand on my back and his lips at my forehead. I fall asleep that way, and wish that I could spend the rest of forever in this little cocoon where I can pretend that my life isn't about to totally implode on itself.

Chapter Twelve

JONATHAN

KITKAT MOCHA

Social Post: We ended up needing to turn this trip into another day, but I didn't want to risk the integrity of the engine. Also, this beauty now has a proper name thanks to my travel companion. Any guesses? #carrestoration #masterscarrestoration #roadtripping #carnames

Image Description: Photo of the car we are bringing from Montana to Colorado.

I wake before the sun comes up, and seeing the puffy redness around Tilly's eyes left behind from her tears breaks my heart. I only heard half of the conversation last night, but it wasn't good. I already wasn't a fan of Tilly's dad based on what little information I had before this trip. I really don't like him now. Not only is he interfering with her plans, her dreams, and her wishes, but now he is affecting the lives of countless others. Pink Every Day is months away from some of the biggest collaborations and launches that they've had so far. And I know, from what Matt and Sasha told me the last time I had dinner with them, that they have some bigger proposals coming in the next two years if everything goes well. I don't think that's going to happen if Tilly's father has his way.

And they don't even know this is potentially coming. Do I need to send Matt a message to give him a heads up or let this play out a bit? I don't want to put Tilly in a harder position than she's already in, but Matt has been one of my best friends since high school. My first loyalty needs to be with him. I need to get more information first, and maybe even help find a different solution.

I find myself placing a soft kiss on Tilly's forehead as I run my fingers through her hair, gently detangling the mess that happened while she slept in my arms. I think she normally sleeps with it braided or tied up in some way, so this exact thing doesn't happen while she's in bed. And I hate that she is going to wake up with this frustration on top of everything else. Gentle strokes and slow movements allow me to detangle most of it before she stirs awake. I'm not sure how long she's been up because as I look down at her, the sleep is gone from her eyes.

"Are you brushing my hair with your fingers?" Her voice is quiet and subdued, and I hate it. I like her to be loud and excited about things. The fatigue is evident in her body and her question and I take a moment to respond to her question and not demand for her to give me her father's phone number so I can sort this out myself. Tilly is a strong, amazing woman. And maybe she just needs me to remind her of that right now. Or at least take her mind off the stress of the last few days.

"I left my comb in my other pants," I murmur softly as I continue my task. Her responding laugh makes me smile.

"Do you really keep combs in your pants?"

"No, but I did find one under a toilet once," I continue, stating it as matter-of-factly as I can. She stirs a bit more, but doesn't pull out of my arms.

"I need to know the story about this." There's a touch of lightness in her voice and I have an internal victory lap over the fact that she's allowing me to distract her.

"When Matt bought his house a few years ago, it needed some significant work inside. Luca and I helped with a lot of it. We wanted to avoid having to pay other people as much as possible, so we got creative and learned a lot as we went. Lots of YouTube videos. Did you know Luca did the dining room furniture for him? Yeah, that was his first dining set. That thing was a pain in the neck to move. Anyway, we were working on the bathroom in the master bedroom ensuite, and when we pulled out the old toilet, there was a comb on the ground by the flange. Apparently, whoever initially installed it ran out of wooden shims and decided to use what they had rather than go get more." By the time I finish, Tilly's cheeks are red with laughter, and she is practically shaking in my arms with the effects of it.

"Please tell me you have a picture of this."

"I think I'm offended that you don't believe me." I pretend to be upset, but she can tell I'm not.

"I believe you. I promise. I just want to see the evidence. Because that's pretty hilarious." I reach behind my back to grab my phone and scroll for a minute to find the photos from Matt's remodel. I don't miss the way she almost buries herself further into my arms with the change in position. She likes being held just as much as I like her being here. My arm might have fallen asleep a few times last night, but it's totally worth it when it comes to getting to hold this beautiful woman in my arms.

"Here it is," I pass her my phone so she can look at the photo and then scroll for a bit if she wants to. I keep talking as she looks.

"That remodel took us the entire summer. It was very likely the hardest thing I've done up until now. Completely worth it, though. I learned a lot that summer, and it gave me the push I needed to start working on older cars, not just at the body shop I had been at up until that point. By the end of the next year, I had gotten enough commissions on the side to put a down payment on my place. And by the next year, I did the same for my sister. I'm halfway done paying for my house now and am on track to have it paid for by the time I'm thirty-five."

"That's amazing. Both of my parents come from old money, so they have lots of assets tied to their names, but I don't know that either has had a blue-collar or physically demanding job. I think my grandfather was a property manager, maybe. I'm not really sure. But I love that you knew what you wanted and worked toward it. Is home remodeling something you would do again? Is that what you want to be when you grow up?" She passes the phone back to me as she settles back in and waits for my answer.

"Honestly, no. Unless it was someone I knew, and they needed help with some things. We made do with what we had, but none of us were experts in the projects we had to do to get that house to the place it is now. Cars are what I'm good at. Especially the vintage ones. I really enjoy that type of work. And whether it's shopping with a buyer to find their perfect next acquisition or replacing a rusted-out frame to its original vision, it's what I love. I plan to retire doing exactly what I'm doing with my life in this moment."

She smiles up at me, and I can tell she has a thousand things running through her head behind her eyes right now. I want to give her an outlet, but I'm not sure where to go with it.

"What do you want to do when you grow up, Tilly?"

"I don't know if I get to choose that for myself anymore."

And the pain and resignation in her tone absolutely breaks my heart. Yeah, that's not going to happen on my watch.

While Tilly showers, I order all the comfort food from room service. Yes, all. I'm going over the budget I set, but I don't care. She needs this. And I need to do this for her. I hate that I couldn't take away her sadness last night, or the defeated look in her gaze this morning. I want to make it all better. But I just don't know how. When she comes out of the bathroom, cheeks rosy from the heat of the shower and hair brushed back into a simple braid, I offer her a smile and show her the spread on the table.

"Did you order everything off the menu?" she chuckles as she places her pajama shirt into her bag and then joins me in the kitchenette area.

"Almost everything. I didn't order the gluten-free pancakes. Figured we could eat the regular ones."

"Perfect." We sit and enjoy the meal together, picking at the different plates and sharing the fruit that was given. I wait until she seems settled before showing her the plan for the day.

"We only have about four hours to go. I'm hoping we get back before noon. Do you want me to bring you to the dorms when we get in, or what would you like if we can make it happen?"

She bites her lip for a moment and then takes a sip of English breakfast tea before responding, "Can we play it by ear? I don't have the mental energy for making decisions right now."

"That's totally fine. If you need to zone out on the ride, that's okay. Or read the whole time. Whatever you want, Tilly. Do you know when your mom is supposed to get you info on the contract?"

"Nope," she pops the 'p' and then sticks her spoon back in her mouth, letting it sit for a moment longer than necessary before she finishes answering, "I hope it's soon because not knowing is driving me crazy."

"If there's anything I can do to help, please let me know."

"Don't make promises you won't be able to keep, Jonathan."

"I never do."

Chapter Thirteen

TILLY

VANILLA BEAN FRAPPUCCINO WITH CHAI

Social Post: Call me basic, but it's sweater weather which means cozy layers, vampy lip colors, and all the chai! #fallincolorado #basicallyme #completelytilly #sweaterweather

Image Description: Selfie of me bundled up in an oversized cream sweater paired with a neutral makeup look but a bold burgundy lippie.

The next six weeks almost passed in a blur. The contract gets read and then sent off to other lawyers, and then read again. We have yet to find a loophole. The only thing that Mom has suggested that may work is asking Dad for an amendment. But what do I even ask him for? I don't know. Right now, the focus is on Sasha and Matt's wedding next weekend. Once we get through that, I can focus on my own thing. And no, I haven't told anyone about the contract marriage that is breathing down my neck. My birthday is January 15th. And I have to be married to

Jason before then. Just great.

Control what you can – that's something Ashley is always saying to herself, and it's a mantra that I've taken up as well. I can't fix this contract thing today. What can I control? I can control my outfit, and dare I say, I look amazing! I'm heading to a new tea shop downtown to spend some time with Ashley, Sasha, and a few other friends before the wedding. She wanted a nighttime coffee event, but we weren't able to make that work. The tea shops, however, were more than happy to host us.

And I was so excited to see this new one! It's partnered with a non-profit, so every event, product, and cup of tea sold goes toward their mission of providing medical supplies and financial support to families who need it. I didn't grow up in a home with a medically complex individual, but I've seen a lot of it in my time in college. Seeing a business practically giving back to their community members calls to me in a way I wasn't expecting. Maybe it's because of what we do at Pink Every Day. This business is doing something similar, in a different demographic and need, but they're still showing up every day to do what they do best. And if I can support that while also filling my tea cabinet – I'm not going to complain.

As I make my way down the hall, I send Jonathan a quick text. Yes, we've been chatting since we got back from the road trip. Nothing fancy. He sends me a picture of his morning smoothie, and I usually show him a daily teacup and book picture. It's our "good morning," and it's become a necessary part of my day. Sometimes the conversation develops more past that and other times, that's enough. Him acknowledging me and being there for me is enough. Those simple pictures feel like his own way of saying that he is there and ready to listen when and if I need to talk.

And today, I took a picture of myself in my full-length mirror before I left my room and decided to send it over. It may be outside of our normal, but I feel amazing tonight. And I have a feeling he's going to appreciate it too. Am I being a bit flirty? Absolutely. Do I regret it? Not a bit.

JONATHAN

The girls are going to a special tea tasting tonight, so the guys are getting together for video games and pizza at Matt's house. Yes, it's pretty basic, but we don't need much. Ashley's fiancé, Marcus, is here, as well as Luca, Matt (obviously), and I. Rowan, one of Ashley's classmates and a friend of Marcus's, is also hanging out with us tonight.

Our group has stayed small, and I'm okay with that. I would have originally thought that Carter would have been here for this, but he decided to royally screw things up with Kylie. And Luca was all too content to wait until she was ready to be more than friends. Marcus is quite a bit older than the rest of us, and Rowan is a bit younger, but we make it work. I'm happy to just sit here and listen to Rowan talk. He's from Scotland, and yes, he has the accent. Marcus was teaching for a while in a university there, but he has a distinct New England accent instead. I think he's originally from Maine. Maybe?

Anyway, I'm taking a break from this round of games to stretch my legs and look at my email. I'm waiting to hear about another special order I made so I can get this next project going. If I'm going to have this car done before December, I need these parts soon. How many times do I need to follow up before they actually get them shipped? I don't want to bug these people, but I have a contract to fulfill, and they told me they would have it done on time. I'm debating calling and leaving a voicemail when a new message notification pops up. I wonder if Tilly's car gave out on her again. My mind drifts a bit before I open it up to see what she might have needed.

And I still haven't said anything to Matt about the contract issues that Tilly is dealing with. In one of our text conversations last week, she asked that I give her until their wedding. And I agreed. There's no reason to stress everyone out if this can potentially be dissolved. Matt knows something has been bothering me though, and I'm pretty sure Luca has picked up on it as well. Even now, I'm getting glances from them from the other room. I know they're wondering why I am not telling them what's bothering me. We'll tell them soon though. Next week.

For now, I have a message to open up from Tilly and I have to force myself to not let my jaw hit the floor when I open do. This girl. She's in a sparkly pink wrap dress. It has a deep V in the front, showing off her gorgeous cleavage. Her hand is in her hair, highlighting just how soft it is. I miss playing with her hair. Her eyes are lined a little heavier than normal, but it makes the color inside pop even more. And of course, she's got on bright pink lipstick. How I wouldn't mind making a mess of that color once she is done taking pictures for the night. The dress ends mid-thigh, showing off the curves I love so much. And of course, she finishes it off with a matching pair of heels. She must have an entire room just for her shoes back at home.

I don't like that thought for some reason. Does Jason know how much this girl loves shoes? Will he give her a hard time about it? Or will he see it as something she loves and give her everything she deserves and more? Will he dote on her like he should? Will he indulge in being an Instagram husband and let her enjoy the things that bring her joy? Or will she be relegated to boozy brunches, yoga classes, and touring preschools even before she's a mother?

I really don't like the thought of that. I take a second to think through my response. Matt comes into the kitchen and stands at the island across from me while I'm debating what I want to say. What's appropriate?

"You good?" he asks as he opens a can of soda and throws his empty one into the recycling bin next to the counter.

"Yeah, question for you though...how did you know you wanted to pursue something with Sasha?"

He chuckles before he responds. "I knew as soon as I saw her. She was perfection, and I wanted to take away all her problems and then be there to make her happy for the rest of my life." I nod, thinking he's done talking, but he isn't. "Why? Are you finally ready to admit that you have a crush on Tilly?" I choke on the water I'd been sipping on as everyone else jerks their heads to make sure I'm okay.

"Yeah, I think I am. And I think it's a bit more than a crush."

I pick up my phone and send her a response. Okay, Jason, let the games begin.

Chapter Fourteen

TILLY

VANILLA COCONUT BLACK TEA

Social Post: Bridal events call for sparkles. #pinkeveryday #pinkeverydayco #bridalshower #bridalevent #sashaloveslipstick

Image Description: Mirror selfie of me in a pink sparkly wrap dress as I head out to Sasha's tea event tonight. Our girl is about to be a married woman!!

Me: <Image Attached>

Five minutes later...

Jonathan: The way you look in that dress should not be allowed.

> Jonathan: You look great, Tilly.
> Have a great time tonight.

When I decided to send Jonathan that picture, I was expecting an emoji reaction, not whatever that was. And I definitely didn't expect my heart to start racing in response. Sure, I felt great, which is why I sent the picture in the first place. But for him to acknowledge that and then tell me? Yeah, wasn't expecting that one. I smile at the message for a solid minute before I put my phone back in my purse and head inside for tea with my girls.

"Well, what's that smile for, hot stuff?" Ashley greets me enthusiastically as I enter the space. It looks like I'm the last one to arrive, and part of me doesn't like that, but the other part of me is okay with it. Because I got to spend a few extra minutes getting ready, which means I feel really good about how I look tonight. And Jonathan apparently appreciates the way I look too. It's taken a long time for me to feel beautiful in the body I have, and knowing he like it too...it has all kinds of flutters happening in my belly.

"Hey, babe. Sorry, I'm just getting here. I wanted to spend a few extra minutes fully getting done up. And someone may have complimented me that I wasn't fully expecting," I give her an 'I'll tell you later' look and I hope she doesn't push it. We can giggle and chat about it later, tonight is about Sasha.

"I'm going to hold you to that, you can hang your coat up over there." She points to an area in the corner with a coat tree and a table with appetizers and multiple teapots. "And then you can pick out your first tea sample. They're going to come out with the bags soon, so we can start playing with our own blends."

The night is sweet and a time to connect with everyone right before the wedding. I haven't said anything to them about what my dad's trying to pull, or what it could mean for us. After Sasha and Matt get married, we can address my problems. I can tell Jonathan wants to tell Matt, but I asked him to wait just a little while longer. One more chance to try to find a way out of this or a few more days for everything to be alright.

For now, I get to make some tea with my friends. And I take my time coming up with a special blend for Jonathan. I can't help it that he's on my mind. He's the only one who knows what the contract is trying to make me do. And it's starting to feel like I don't have any other option. I'm not ready to get married, especially to a guy that I don't really know.

"Control what you can, Tilly," I whisper to myself as I get my things together to leave the tea shop and head back to my dorm room. I can't change the contract. But I can make the best of the situation. I can continue to support my friends. I can keep focusing on my classes and those around me. I can help make sure that Sasha's special day is everything she deserves. And I can start working on a plan to work around this contract after this weekend.

It isn't until that night, when I'm lying in bed, staring at my heels on the floor that I wore tonight, and the bag from the tea house – holding the blend I made for Jonathan – that I have an idea of how we may be able to work around this contract. I have to at least try.

> Me: Do the lawyers still think we might be able to get something added to the contract in order to stay compliant, but let me have a little more control?

> Mom: Yes, your dad has asked that you call him at your earliest convenience though. I know you have the wedding this weekend, but he's getting impatient. I don't want him to show up and make a scene for you. Don't wait too long. I love you.

> Me: Love you too, Mom. Thank you.

> Mom: No thanks necessary, Tilly. Chat soon.

The next morning, I put on my favorite casual outfit. It may just be jeans and a cute top, but they fit me perfectly. And I need to feel good right now. Because I'm about to ask the man that is fast becoming one of my best friends to marry me in order to save everything I've been helping to build for the last four years. No biggie. I got this.

Classes finish, and I get all of the work done that's on my list for myself and then for Pink Every Day. We are doing a lot of wedding content this week, and it just helps solidify what I need to do. I have to do everything I can to save this company. I just hope it works. Here goes nothing.

> Me: Hey, I made you something last night. Can I swing by the shop to give it to you? Not sure how late you are working this afternoon.

> Jonathan: Hi. Yeah, I'm here until five today. Come on by. Did you have fun last night?

> Me: I did. What about you?

> Jonathan: Had a good time. Pretty chill, but perfect. I just had a client walk in, so I have to go, but I'll see you when you get here. I don't have anyone else stopping by for appointments, so whenever works for your schedule should work for me. See you soon.

> Me: See you soon.

An hour later, I'm walking into the shop to see Jonathan – the tea blend I made for him and the biggest favor I've ever asked for in my life in hand. Here goes nothing.

13

• June

• Wednesday

2:00 *tail light replacement*

165-201

• Week · 24

July

Chapter Fifteen

JONATHAN

PINK CHAI

Social Post: Don't knock it until you try it. This is incredible.
#nocofinds #foco #fortcollinstea #tryingsomethingnew

Image Description: Iced pink chai in a clear cup sitting on an outdoor table.

The bell above the door dings, and I look up from my computer screen to see Tilly walking into the shop. She looks nervous, but still insanely gorgeous.

"Hey, pretty girl. How's your day going?" I can't help the smile that takes over my face as I take her in. Pink is definitely her color. The lightweight sweater she is wearing shows off her curves, and I love that she is comfortable in her body, because it's incredible.

"Pretty good. I made you something." She approaches the desk and hands me the brown paper bag with a familiar logo on the outside.

"Made? I didn't realize you were going to get to make your own blends of tea last night. What did you make for me?" I open the bag enough that I can look at the contents inside as well as smell the leaves, trying to figure out what she added to something she made. With me in mind. On purpose.

"It's a combination of green and white teas, and then I added some peony petals too," she waits a beat before continuing, and I realize she's waiting for my approval or encouragement to continue. I take a moment to smell the leaves inside the bag and am overwhelmed with a sense of comfort and rightness.

"I can't wait to try this. I didn't know peonies were used in tea making," I smell the leaves again. I really need to get some additional things in here so I can make tea in the office. I don't want to wait until I get home to have a cup of this. The fact she made it specifically for me just makes it that much better.

"Yeah, not very common, but they are. I actually picked them because of their meaning," she hurries to continue, probably already knowing my next question. "Most flowers have cultural or symbolic meanings. There's actually a full study behind the symbolism of flowers. It's fascinating. Anyway, peonies have several meanings, but there are a few that pop up in most floriography blogs. New beginnings, prosperity and happiness, and a happy marriage."

I don't catch my reaction in time, and my face falls. "So, you've decided to go ahead and marry Jason? Is that what *you* want to do?"

She hurries to respond before I can fully process my feelings about that revelation anymore, "No, I don't want to marry Jason. I left that life for a reason. And I don't want to go back. I just can't do this on my own."

"So, what are you wanting to do? I know you wanted to wait until after Sasha and Matt's wedding to really start making a game plan and to tell them what's happening. Did you change your mind?"

"I know this is absolutely crazy and feel free to say 'no,' because I'm fully aware of how insane this sounds."

"What is it, Tilly? I told you, if there's anything I can do to help with this, I want to make it happen." If she's ready to ask for my help, I hope it's something I can fulfill. I want to take this situation away for her, make everything all better so she can go back to the happy, full of life person I know her to be.

"I need to see if Dad will accept it as an amendment to the contract, but if he does, will you marry me, Jonathan?"

I know I stare at her for longer than would be considered appropriate, but I need to make sure I heard that right. I replay the question over in my head once, twice, and again before I respond.

"Did you just - propose to me in the middle of my auto body shop?"

She smiles softly at me, hope evident in every ounce of her person, "Yes, I did. Don't make me get down on one knee because I don't have a ring, and these are my good jeans, and I don't want to get any oil on them." Not that she would get oil on her jeans, we are in the receptionist side of things and we keep the floor immaculately clean over here. I know this isn't as black and white as we are making it seem in this moment. It would be a contract marriage. She's being required to do this because of business requirements and obligations that her dad is placing on her. This isn't going to be a cutesy little arrangement; there will be stipulations and meetings.

Will I be able to keep all of my own assets? Will her dad want access to my business? My home? My sister's home? I know this is going to complicate things, but I want the chance to get to know Tilly better – to show her that I am the right choice for her. Just like she's always whispering to herself, I bring to mind her saying – Control what you can. I can't control her dad. But I can control my response to her questions.

"Well, in that case, Tilly Chance, I would be honored to marry you." I want to kiss her. Am I allowed to kiss her? Probably not. She asked me because I'm her friend. She knows me. She trusts me.

"Good, okay. There's a lot of logistics we need to talk through, but I need to see if Dad will take this as an option first. Would you be able to get together a list of your assets and any other reasons you can think of to give my dad to say 'yes' to this? And we can chat on my dad's proposed terms and our own terms after Sasha and Matt's wedding is over. Does that work?"

"I can make that work."

This may just be trading one contract marriage for another, but

I am not going to turn it down. I can be her husband if that's what she needs. Not only will this potentially save our friend's careers and dreams, but this can put Tilly in a much better spot as well. And I'll cross my fingers each and every day that she wants to turn this into more. Because I think I already love the gorgeous woman standing in front of me.

   With Matt and Sasha's wedding in just a few days, and Tilly trying to figure out things on the back end with her mom and lawyers, I'm just kind of...waiting, which is not my strong suit. I wish I had something I could do, especially since it's going to be a very quick turnaround if we actually make this work. Her birthday is January 15th, which means we would have to get married before then. And she's probably going to have to move in with me if this is going to be an actual arrangement like what her dad wants. I don't want to be presumptuous, but it would be a lot easier to show her that I want something real with her if she's sleeping in my house every night.

   I end up spending the rest of the day cleaning out the largest spare room in my house. Luckily, it has a full ensuite and a walk-in closet. I just need to see if I can get some additional shelving installed to accommodate her shoes. I'm not sure if she is a shoe box or display person when it comes to them, but I want her to have options, so I add it to my mental list to ask Ashley how she stored her shoes while they were roommates. The fall air is crisp and brings the perfect amount of chill in the breeze. My fingers may be a little cold by the time I'm done, but the room is clean and aired out, and I'm ready to ask her what she would want for furnishings and linens in this space, because this is going to be hers.

   Now, to work on the rest of the house so she can be comfortable here. Something that I wasn't expecting when I started working on vintage cars is the price that comes with doing that kind of work. The parts are expensive, but so is the knowledge, skill, and labor to get the work done. And with Matt's help, I invested quite a bit of my initial capital that came in from the beginning projects. Which means I have a four-bedroom house in Windsor that is well on its way to being paid off. I may not be as well off as the family Tilly's dad would like her to marry into, but I have enough to treat her like the queen she is. Now I just need to get the okay from the lawyers on all fronts before I go and drop some money on a ring I know she's going to love.

She may have been the one to ask me to marry her, but I will be the one pursuing her from this moment forward. And that starts with finding the little things that show her just how much she means to me. How much I see her, hear her, value her. And that she is worth every single second of my time and attention. Time to make some phone calls.

Chapter Sixteen

TILLY

MAPLE PUMPKIN MOCKTAIL

Social Post: Wedding day is here and done. One more chapter is completed in Sasha's story and I am honored that I got to be a part of it. #weddingday #sashaloveslipstick #pinkeverydayco #pinkeveryday #coloradobride

Image Description: Selfie with me and Sasha – she's all married!!

Sasha and Matt's wedding day was spectacular! I was in the wedding party, but I'm also handling the social media, posting sneak peeks for Sasha's accounts and for Pink Every Day to show off the details and send our company's congratulations.

While the guests dance and enjoy themselves, I take a few moments to breathe and just watch. The content didn't take long to get up, but it's nice to take a few minutes to see how happy everyone is. Part of me is so scared that it's all about to fall apart. They have no idea of the threat my father has made toward everything Sasha and the rest of us have been building. I asked Jonathan to wait until after the wedding to bring anything up, but now I feel like that might not have been the best move. I'm going to pop her happy bubble as soon as it finishes forming.

Is it so bad to want them to enjoy their happiness for as long as possible? I just want to make sure she doesn't lose it all. At least, I hope I have a decent backup plan. Jonathan is a good guy, and if it goes well, I'll get to make sure Pink Every Day is set up for stable and long-term success while sharing a house with someone who is quickly growing to be my best friend. I can be Mrs. Jonathan Masters. I like the sound of that. My phone starts buzzing on the table just as I decide to hit the dance floor again. With everything happening, I can't ignore it.

And before you ask, yes, I did change my dad's name in my phone. I was annoyed. Don't judge.

> Sperm Donor: You and your mother have been gone long enough. It's time to come home. Jason is expecting you home for Christmas, and you have an engagement party to plan. We have an agreement, Tilly. Don't make me come get you.

Here's my chance, fingers crossed.

> Me: What are the chances that we can amend the agreement?

> Sperm Donor: Unless you plan on getting married to someone of equal caliber before December, I expect you home and ready to comply by December 5th.

> Me: Okay.

I open a new message string.

> Me: Dad is open to amending the agreement. Can you have the lawyers draw up the documents and send them over? I'd like to get this nailed down this weekend. I can't let Dad do this, and I don't want to become someone's pretty little wife waiting at home for the next five years of my life.

Mom: Who have you lined up to be your husband?

I glance up and immediately make eye contact with Jonathan across the dance floor. He's holding a glass with a sparkling drink inside, a soft smile on his face. In my eyes, I must be asking a million questions, but he sees them all. A gentle nod is all the confirmation from him that I need.

> Me: Jonathan Masters. We need to be married before December 5th. Dad moved up the deadline.

> Mom: I'll get back to you when they let me know what they need. I love you, Tilly. Now go have fun at the wedding.

> Me: Love you too, Mom. Thanks.

"So, do we have the green light with your plan?" Jonathan asks as he sits next to me, setting his drink down and draping his suit jacket over my shoulders. I didn't even realize he took it off, or that I was getting cold. This man picks up on my subtle shifts in posture and emotions better than I do sometimes.

"I think so. Mom is getting with the lawyers to go over specifics, and we should have the first round of contracts to read over sometime tomorrow. Are you sure you're okay with this? What happens if you meet someone over the next few years? I don't want you putting your life on hold because my dad is a jerk and has to throw a temper tantrum each time he doesn't get his way."

"You're not putting my life on hold, Tilly. I want to help. And I have a feeling that being married to you isn't going to be any kind of imposition." I look up at him to make sure he's not joking, and then have to giggle when he literally winks at me. Yes, the man winked at me. And I'm blushing again.

"I do have a question for you, though," he says, taking another sip of his drink before pulling out his phone.

"What's up?"

"Does noon tomorrow work for you to have an appointment with me?"

"Um, I think I'm free all day tomorrow. What kind of appointment?"

"We're going ring shopping, pretty girl. If we are doing this, we're doing it right."

The man picks me up in the prettiest car I have ever seen in my life! Seriously, though, I have no clue what it is or when he got it, but it's gorgeous. And how many cars does he even have? Maybe he rented it...or borrowed it, honestly, that's not important right now.

I stayed at Ashley's house last night so I didn't have to drive to and from the venue myself. And if Ashley thought it was weird that Jonathan was picking me up this morning, she didn't say anything. I did get a bit of a look of "you're going to tell me about this later," and a shared giggle before I closed the front door behind me. Not only does he park right in front of the house so I can go straight from the sidewalk to the car, but he steps out and comes to open my door for me. Breaking news, ladies: Chivalry is not dead; it just needs some encouragement sometimes.

"Why, thank you. Mr. Masters," I offer a mock curtsey before settling into the seat. He waits until I'm fully inside before gently closing the door and jogging around to the other side. I look to the house in time to see Ashley and Marcus at the big picture window in front, giving a wave to Jonathan and a mouthed "oh my gawd" from Ashley to me. I know, right??

"Not a problem, Miss Chance. Oh, I have this for you," I don't know why I'm surprised. He does this every time I see him earlier in the day. But he hands me a smoothie in a travel container.

"Thank you. What did you make for me today?"

"It's a blue coconut smoothie. It has protein powder in it as well as maca and spirulina, so lots of productive calories. I'm new to using maca – it's actually a root vegetable, but it has a surprising number of benefits. You'll have to let me know what you think. And that blend of everything should leave you full for a good portion of the morning. At least until we finish our errands, anyway."

"Are we going to more than one place? I thought we were going to look at rings and then call it a day…" I take a sip before I finish my thought, and then have to stop because this is too good.

"Do you like surprises?"

"Only the good ones."

"These are good ones. We are doing rings first, and then we have a few more stops to make before lunch with Sasha, Matt, and the rest of the group. They're not leaving for their honeymoon yet, so they asked if we wanted to do lunch with them and the others today."

"I must have missed that memo. Wait, they asked you if *we* wanted to? They knew we were hanging out?"

"I talked to Matt a little bit this week about what's going on. Nothing specific. But I may have told him that we were talking about pursuing something more than friends and seeing what would happen. I wasn't sure how much you wanted to tell everyone, but I didn't want it to be a massive shock if they came back from their honeymoon and we were full-on engaged."

"That makes sense. Okay, let's go get things done then. Also, this smoothie is fantastic."

"I thought you might like it." We sit in comfortable silence until we get to the jewelry store. A very nice jewelry store in downtown Windsor. I unbuckle, but Jonathan rests his hand on my thigh for a moment in a gesture to still me and tell me to wait before I climb out, not gonna lie, I don't hate his hands on me like this. "I have just one rule for today."

"Okay, what's up?" I hold his gaze as he searches my eyes for something.

"You aren't allowed to pay for anything, or offer to pay for anything today. I want to do this. Every bit of this with you, Tilly. I told you I'm here to help, to be there for you, and that starts today. I'm a full-grown adult with a big boy job and a house. I manage my money and my time well. And I will never offer something that I am not willing to give or to make happen. Okay?" The seriousness of his tone and what he is asking of me takes me aback a little bit. I was not expecting this level of control from Jonathan. He tends to be a bit quieter, like Matt. Very sure of himself, but content to just watch and go with the flow.

But in this moment, he is the one setting the pace. And he's asking me to trust him.

"I can do that." He links his fingers with mine and then raises the back of my hand to his lips. Placing a gentle kiss on my skin and a wake of goosebumps all the way up my arm, he smiles at me in acknowledgment.

"Good, now let's go pick you out something as beautiful as you are."

Who is this man right now??

13

- June

- Wednesday

2:00 *tail light replacement*

Chapter Seventeen

JONATHAN

BLUE COCONUT SMOOTHIE

Social Post: Today's agenda looks a little different than my normal... yes, this is a teaser and no, you don't get any more information yet. #myday #masterscarrestoration #noco

Image Description: Lit up jewelry counter.

Walking into the jewelry store could have been fairly overwhelming. Luckily, I've worked with one of the sales associates before when I was picking out some jewelry for my mom and sister last year. So, I was able to give her a call and ask for a private appointment as well as a pre-selected spread for Tilly to look through first.

If she doesn't like any of these, we will move on, but I have a feeling she will find something that suits her perfectly. And this is just our first stop of the day, so I don't want her to get decision fatigue over everything. Limited choices are best. And I am happy

to ensure she only has the best options to choose from. It helps that I already know her pretty well. Not as well as Matt knew Sasha when he started wooing her, but not too far off.

"Welcome back, Mr. Masters. I trust your morning has gone well so far," Stacia, the salesperson, greets us as we walk to her counter in the back of the store.

"Yes, thank you, Stacia. This is Tilly, my fiancée," I motion in introduction and don't miss the slight pink of Tilly's cheeks at the title I give her. "We'd love to see what you picked out for us to look through today. Did you find the Art Deco pieces that I requested?" Tilly seems almost surprised at the conversation, but I'm happy to show her that I'm not just the guy who works on cars.

"Yes, sir. I've pulled a variety for you to review. I believe this was the one you specifically asked to see."

I know the moment Tilly set her eyes on the piece. And that it is going to be the one we will be leaving the jewelers with. It has an emerald as the center stone, cushioned with pavé diamonds and silver filigree work. It is a stunning piece, and one that I noticed the last time I was in with my mom to get a new watch battery. Yes, she is that person that still goes into the jeweler to get her watch battery replaced instead of doing it herself at home, and I love her for it. I immediately thought of Tilly when I saw it. I didn't know then that I would have the chance to give it to her, to use it to ask her to take my name and be a part of my life, but here we are.

"Oh, that's stunning. Can I try it on?" Her eyes were wide, and if she were a Disney princess, there would probably be birds singing and sewing her wedding dress in response to it.

"Absolutely. Mr. Masters has immaculate taste in jewelry selection. The pieces he has picked out in the past for his mom and sister have been some of my favorites, too. And now it looks like we get to add you to that list."

"It's stunning. And it fits perfectly. I've never seen a piece like this." Tilly's hushed statement speaks to the awe she has for it.

"Would you like to see the wedding band that goes with it?" Stacia asks, and Tilly looks to me first before nodding. The simple silver band fits next to the engagement ring perfectly. It has a row of pavé diamonds inset in the band along with a few emeralds to accent the color. It's a bold set together, but still elegant. It's something that I can see her wearing and cherishing for thirty or forty years before passing it along to our own daughter. This is where memories happen and traditions begin. And I find that I want to create a thousand of those moments with her.

"What about you? We need to pick out a band for you, too." Tilly's statement surprises me. I figured I'd get something at some point, but I wanted today to be about her.

"We can do that later. No huge rush."

"We're here now, and I know you have plans, so if we can't stay, I get that, but I'd like to look if we have time." I glance at my watch before meeting her gaze again.

"We have time."

Thirty minutes later, I have two ring boxes in a white linen package from the jeweler, and Tilly has a gorgeous new "sparkly" on her finger and the biggest smile on her face.

"What's next?" she asks as she gets settled into her seat next to me.

"We have a wedding registry appointment in twenty minutes, so enough time on the drive over for you to start thinking about how you want to decorate, what you will need at the house, if there's anything you need to look up, all that fun stuff." I pull onto the main road and start making my way to the other side of town.

"I think between what you already have and what I have, we should be okay. Do we really need to ask people for things?"

I rest my hand on the center console, trying to remind myself that I don't have permission to touch her yet, even though I so desperately want to settle her and reassure her that everything is okay.

"It's not just for people to buy things. It'll be an easy way for you to build your dream home, in a sense. And then, we can go back to the house and you can decide what you want to adjust on the list or remove it fully. Your dad and his society friends and acquaintances will expect certain things. That includes asking for a new China set even though I already have one, and we probably won't ever have a reason for a thirty-person dinner service, but it's expected."

"You have a China set already?"

"I love that's what you picked up on from that. But yes, my grandmother had two sets, and my sister and I each received one when she passed away a few years ago. It's a classic pattern, and you might love it. So, think of a second one as the display ones or the ones we'll use. Whatever you prefer is fine with me. But I want you to go crazy, pick what your dream items would be. If you want all of the knobs on the cabinetry to be hand-carved Aspen and then dipped in gold, let's add it to the list. You come from a high-society space. And even though I know you love the simple things and the little moments of beauty, this is the expectation. Don't give your dad a reason to think that you are settling for anything less than you deserve."

"I wish I could write that down." Her smile is genuine, and I love the way her eyes brighten as she takes it all in, knowing that I meant everything I just said.

"I have no problem reminding you every day."

By the time we are on our way to lunch, I can tell Tilly is approaching her limit of decision-making. The fatigue is evident on her face, even though she is doing her best to power through. It's a lot. We were able to make it through most of the registry stuff before I told her we would come back to finish later. With everything for the kitchen, dining room, and bathrooms picked out, I'm happy that we needed to take a pause. And we'll be able to go back on Tuesday after she gets out of classes to do the bedrooms, her office space, and choose our outdoor items. If nothing else, I now have a really good handle on her style and what she wants to see in our home.

"So, what do you want to tell everyone when we get to lunch? I'm happy to go along with whatever, but I want you to be comfortable. We can wait until Sasha and Matt get back from their honeymoon to fill them in on all the details going on with the contracts, but I'd like to tell them the basics of what we will be doing." We are about five minutes away, and I hate putting her on the spot, but we need to have a plan here so she doesn't feel awkward if something comes up. And something will come up, considering the ring on her finger.

"Can we wait until someone asks what's going on, and then we can say my dad has put some stipulations on things that I needed to figure out, and you're helping me. We are already good friends, so this is your classic 'marriage of convenience' story."

"Another romance novel reference, I'm guessing?"

"Exactly. We just won't give the details of the evil mayor forcing his daughter to choose between her own happiness and that of her best friends and everything we've been building. And I'm not saying I won't be happy with you – I just wish this was allowed to happen organically if it was going to happen. Not that I'm mad about it. But...I'm totally not saying what I want to say here, am I?"

I forget for a moment that we aren't in an actual relationship, and I reach over to grab her hand, holding it in mine, giving her that bit of reassurance that I see her and I'm here. "You're okay, Tilly. I know what you mean. I'm not mad about this either. I know he put you in a terrible position, and I can't even imagine all that you have been working through these past few months trying to figure it out. I'm here and I'm yours for as long as you'll have me."

And with that, I place another gentle kiss on the back of her hand and park the car. "Let's do this then."

Chapter Eighteen

TILLY

GINGER PEAR MOCKTAIL

Social Post: Look at them all married!! #brunch #afterparty #sashaloveslipstick

Image Description: Sasha and Matt sharing a quick kiss at brunch this morning.

"I feel like we don't have the full story here," Ashley points her finger at Jonathan and then at me, back and forth a few times. She's the only other one in the group that kind of knows the story with my parents. Not all of it, but enough to know that there is probably more that we aren't sharing. I've kept much of my pre-Colorado life to myself since forming these friendships. It's not filled with fun memories that I like to revisit, and no one likes listening to people complain about being a wealthy teenager.

"I need you to be okay with this and our answer for now. Maybe we will be able to share more later, but at this point this is all I can give you. This might not have been our first choice or how we would have wanted this all to go, but we are happy, and we are settling into what this is going to look like. And we could really use your support as we jump into this. Especially since we have a tight timeline." I answer her, stirring my little straw in the iced tea in front of me, waiting for all of our closest friends to question us further or accept what we need.

"Okay, so, when is the wedding date?" Sasha asks, giving us her full support. I couldn't be happier right now. This group, these people, have become my home, my family. I couldn't do life without them.

"I didn't mean to steal any of your excitement from your wedding, Sasha. If we could have picked better timing for this, we would have."

Sasha shushes me before I'm able to continue rambling further.

"That didn't even cross my mind, Tilly. You're part of our family. And I know you wouldn't do something to maliciously hurt anyone. This is life right now, and that's okay."

"As for a date, we aren't sure yet. We have to wait a bit to make sure everything goes through with her dad, and then we will go from there. We'll let you know as soon as we have that information, though. We do know it will be before December 5th." Jonathan offers in answer as I try to hold back the tears. I don't deserve these people. My phone buzzes as I half listen to the others offer suggestions for a place to have the ceremony and if we want an engagement party, and when Jonathan wants to start moving my stuff into the house.

> Mom: Everything is good to go. You'll need to have Jonathan sign the contract that has been emailed to him, and then you'll need to do the same. You need to have the ceremony before December 5th, and your dad and I would both like to be in attendance. I understand if this ends up being an elopement, though. You will need to stay married for five full years in order for Jonathan to inherit your father's shares in the two companies of his choosing. There are a few other changes based on you marrying Jonathan and not Jason. Please let me know if you need anything revised.

"The contract has been adjusted, and we each have a copy in our emails. Ready to do this?" I ask Jonathan quietly and then show him the message from my mom.

"Let's set a date and get married," he answers with the most genuine smile I have ever seen on his face.

"How does the last Saturday in November sound?"

"I think I can make that work."

The next few weeks are busier than I could have possibly imagined. Classes are a whirlwind of preparing for projects, tests, and working around stipulations to make sure I can have everything completed before our wedding day. I am still staying in the dorms, allowing Jonathan to get some remodeling done on the house. He was right, of course, and the items that stayed on our registry were quickly purchased by my father's friends. My dad also paid to have some upgrades done on Jonathan's house. Nothing that was actually necessary, but Dad would not be dissuaded. I was upset at first, but then my fiancé (love that word by the way) said that we can give this to him because there would be plenty over the next five years that we would not want him to have any say in.

"Control what you can and leave the rest." I would say out loud every time things started feeling like they were starting to spiral. And each time, Jonathan would lace his fingers with mine and then place a gentle kiss on the back of my hand.

"Exactly."

The house wasn't ever a 'bachelor pad,' yet it's definitely feeling more like a home now. We decided on colors and patterns that feel reminiscent of the Greek restaurant we visited on our road trip. Soft blues, navy, whites, and creams make up the color palette. It's soothing and clean while still feeling homey. Adding some statement pieces that Luca had in his shop for both furniture and decor really made the place feel like ours. And even though our relationship isn't a physical one, it still feels kind of weird setting up my own bedroom in our home. But I need that separation, that space that can be my own. Did I mention I can actually have my shoes out too? The walk-in closet in my bedroom has these amazing shelves that hold all my heels in a way that I can easily see them, but they aren't in the way of my clothes. Plus, I have a full home office too. And it might be more amazing than the space for my shoes.

We opted to skip an engagement party and are planning to do a reception back home over the semester break. I didn't want to spend my birthday back around my dad, but I know it's going to be expected for us to make an appearance. I can give him this. The actual ceremony will be simple. I have a beautiful white cocktail-type dress that is flattering, but not too formal. And I can wear it again for the reception later on. We still need to decide on a place, though.

"We're keeping it pretty small. What do you think about the tea house?" Jonathan asks as we have a dinner of grilled chicken, rice, and roasted broccoli one night at the beginning of November. I've been coming over for dinner twice a week as we get closer to making things official. It's allowed us time to spend together as well as do the preparations on the house and for the wedding, too. Even with it being an intimate affair, there are still a few little details that I want to be perfect. My dad is coming out for this, the first time seeing my life out here, and I want him to see this as serious work and not just me playing with makeup.

"I love that idea. The space is beautiful. I was debating something outside, but I have no clue what the weather will be like. I'll give the event coordinator a call tomorrow and see if they have the date free. If they do, I'll book a full rental. Is that okay with you?"

"Sounds great. How's everything going with classes this semester? I know you had to bump up a few things so you could be done before the wedding. Is there anything I can help with, or are you in a good spot with your workload?"

"I think I'm okay. I had a lighter course load this semester, so there wasn't much I had to work around. How is the work on the Shelby coming?"

"Really good, actually. The buyer said that part of the deal on his end is shifting, but he still wanted me to get the work done. He's actually picking it up the day before the wedding. And that's my last big job of the year, so I'll be able to fully take time off for December until you start your new semester of classes. I know we didn't really talk about it, but I'm assuming you want to finish your last semester in the spring?" Jonathan finishes his last bite and waits for me to answer. I love these moments that we can converse with each other – catching up on all the things going on in our lives, what we want to do in the coming months, and just being together. It's simple and it's perfect. Just what I need right now.

"I do. I know the contract specifies that I need to be fulfilling the tasks required of me at home as a priority, and that's something I wouldn't be surprised if Dad shows up randomly to make sure I'm not letting the house fall apart, and that I'm cooking dinners for you regularly. But I do really want to step into this role with Sasha and Pink Every Day. I can't imagine doing anything else, not right now anyway." Before I even finish speaking, he's reaching across the table to hold my hand, giving me that quiet reassurance that he hears what I'm saying and that he has my back on it. I'm never going to feel alone with this man by my side.

For a moment, I allow myself to feel the fear and overwhelm that comes to mind. What happens if he decides this is too much?

119

What if dad decides to sabotage my career a different way? What if? The questions will keep coming unless I stop it here. So, I take a deep breath and focus on the feel of Jonathan's fingers laced with my own. He is here now. With me. By choice and on purpose. And I have to trust that he won't be the one to walk away from this arrangement.

Jonathan: Thinking of you this morning. You're going to do great on your exam! Call me if you need anything, and I'll chat with you after classes.

Me: Thank you. I have on my favorite yellow shoes, so I'm ready to make today amazing.

Jonathan: LOL. Do I get to see?

Me: Why, Mr. Masters, are you flirting with me?

Jonathan: Would that be so bad?

I stare at my phone for a moment analyzing his question. I'm not totally oblivious and know that he's been dropping some not so subtle hints that he likes me. As more than a friend. But is it just infatuation or harmless flirting, or is he looking for something more? Adding feelings into things, at least the stage we are in right now, is going to add a whole new layer of complications to things. That's a conversation for another day when I'm not running to class though. I decide to send him the picture I took in the mirror this morning along with a brief text before pocketing my phone and continuing to walk to class.

Me: Sending you a bit of sunshine.
<winky face emoji>

I feel the buzz of another text or two, but I ignore them. I need to get in the right headspace for this test. I can overthink whether Jonathan is actually seeing me as more than his fake fiancée and how I feel about that possibility later. Priorities, Tilly.

The next morning, I have my first class of the day with Professor Williams, who also happens to be Ashley's fiancé. It's still a daily struggle to remember to call him Professor when I'm on campus, and that I'm allowed to call him Marcus when we are hanging out as friends. I give him a little wave as I enter the classroom and find a spot off to the side to get settled. This one is a longer lecture, and I need to see if I have something to eat in my backpack. Because yes, I forgot to eat this morning. And I don't have time to run to a vending machine or the coffee cart to get something before class starts. Of course, I don't have anything with me. I'm debating texting Ashley to see if she wants to swing by to surprise her man with breakfast while he's teaching, when he walks over to my seat.

"I was asked to deliver this to you, Miss Chance," he tells me as he hands me a travel cup and a brown paper bag.

"Oh, thank you. Where did this come from?" I take the items from him and set them on my lap, peeking inside the bag to see a blueberry muffin, and it smells incredible!

"Mr. Masters dropped it off on his way into work this morning. He's only a couple of streets down from my house, so I think he wanted to make sure you got taken care of on a day when he couldn't do it directly." He offers a smile and then goes to the front of the classroom to begin the lecture.

I take a quick sip and immediately know that it's another one of Jonathan's signature smoothies. And knowing him, there's probably extra protein and something for immune support in here, too. I think his love languages are feeding people, providing, and caring for them. Because he has gone above and beyond in every single area. I mentioned to him once that I liked flavored honeys to mix up my plain black teas in the morning. The next time I was over at the house, there were literally ten different flavored honeys added to the tea cabinet. He also had an entire printout on the ideal pairings for those honey flavors with teas.

> Me: Thank you for my breakfast. It's perfect.

> Jonathan: You're welcome, Tilly. Have a good day.

> Me: I'm feeling very spoiled over here. LOL.

> Jonathan: Just doing what I can to take care of you. :)

> Me: You're doing an amazing job.

> Jonathan: I appreciate the positive feedback. Now, put the phone away and pay attention. I'll chat with you tonight.

And I can't help the smirk that takes over my face at the way he's continuing to take care of me.

13

· June

· Wednesday

2:00 tail light replacement

165 201

· Week 24

Chapter Nineteen

JONATHAN

BANANA MATCHA SMOOTHIE

Social Post: I'm almost done working on this gorgeous car. It's been such a fun project and a highlight to complete. #classiccars #masterscarrestoration #shelby #commissionedwork #carcollectors

Image Description: Tape on the hood of the Shelby as I get ready for the final paint touch ups.

Going from not being in any sort of relationship to being engaged to be married in a matter of weeks is quite the status change. The house is all ready for Tilly to move in. I'm almost done working on this car for Clark, and I'm looking forward to having some time off. December is going to be busy with traveling to see Tilly's family and getting settled into our new life together. We are only a week away from the wedding at this point, and not going to lie, I'm getting a little nervous about meeting her dad. I haven't heard much good about the man, but he's been happy to throw money at my house to make sure it's everything Tilly could possibly need or want. I had the money to get the work done myself, but he was pretty insistent on contributing.

I haven't even talked to him directly over the phone yet. Primarily communicating through his staff and email, the relationship has been very professional. And while some side comments have been made that tell me he isn't thrilled with me being a blue-collar trade worker, I'm doing what I love. And if he has a problem with that, well, he doesn't have to come out for more check-ins than what's already planned. The level to which he micromanages everything is astounding. I can't even imagine growing up like this. No wonder Tilly is always waiting to be told that what she's doing isn't the right decision. If only showing her that she does have her own agency was as simple as picking out her engagement ring or the new paint for the exterior siding of the house.

"Uncle Jonathan!!" I hear yelling just as I turn off the blender. My front door closes, and I hear running as the boys head into the kitchen, followed closely by my sister, Alayne.

"Thank you again so much for taking them this morning. I got called in early, and I know it isn't on our schedule, but I was close to having to take them with me to work." Alayne sets their lunch boxes on the table alongside their hats and gloves. If I had to guess, Shane and Henry didn't want to layer up this morning, but they are definitely going to want them when they get to school. We really need to do a fundraiser to get the HVAC system updated. Half of the classrooms don't adequately heat, and the other half don't ever actually cool down once it gets to the warmer months. Not exactly conducive to learning.

"Don't worry about it. I'm here and available, and I'm more than happy to help." I set a glass of the smoothie concoction for the day in front of both of my nephews and then pass my sister a travel cup. She's like a lot of moms out there and forgets to actually take care of herself in the midst of caring for the boys, juggling home and work responsibilities.

"Oh good, food." She happily takes the cup and then kisses her kids on the tops of their heads before scurrying out the door. The door has barely closed behind her before I start getting the barrage of questions that come with kids.

"So, why don't we get to be in the wedding?" Shane, the older of the two, asks me.

"Yeah, I know we aren't old enough to be groomsman, but this is the first wedding we are being allowed to attend. I want a job," Henry adds to his brother's sentiment. I just laugh a little before setting my own sipped-on glass down on the marble countertop that they are sitting at.

"It's going to be pretty small. None of our friends are standing up with us. We would rather everyone enjoy the day and be there are our family. And if you had jobs to do, you wouldn't be able to enjoy it as much." They take a moment to think over my explanation before they nod in agreement. I guess that was the only answer they needed.

"Are you guys going on a honeymoon?" Shane asks, and I wonder when he decided to get so very interested in all the things that happen during a wedding.

"Not quite yet, we need to go visit Tilly's dad for a reception with his friends during the semester break. Once she finishes classes and graduates in May, we may see about doing some traveling. It all depends on what is going to happen with her role at Pink Every Day and what my workload looks like."

"You should take her to Greece!" Henry pipes up, finishing his glass and then drawing with the condensation on the counter. This boy is always drawing something, but he much prefers when he can do it tactically, like charcoal, chalks, or apparently, water.

"And why would that be the chosen destination?" I love these talks I have with my nephews. They aren't full-grown yet, but I know it's going to happen before any of us are ready for it. And I love hearing their reasons and explanations for things. Their minds work incredibly to form connections and relationships between what they see and what they know – and think they know.

"Well, isn't that what this entire remodel is themed after?" Shane asks in a 'this should be obvious' way as he glances around the kitchen and dining space.

"You're right. It is. How did you make the connection with Greece, though?"

"Probably the color scheme – it matches the flag of the country. And you have a few new books on the coffee table that talk about Greek culture and architecture. It wasn't hard to figure out."

"You pay attention to so much, I'm not sure why I thought I could get that past you."

"I see everything," Shane waves his fingers in a spooky sort of way as he says that, and both his brother and I start laughing. I love these kids so much.

"Okay, grab your stuff. Let's get you guys to school."

After dropping them off, I head down to the shop. I am almost done with Clark's car and want to take it on a final test drive to make sure everything is working properly before I call him to come take a look. I'll need to wait until rush hour and the regular commuters get where they need to be, though. There's no way I'm taking this car on the road with people running late and distracted parents trying to yell over Baby Shark on their way to daycare to drop off their toddlers for another day.

Angel, my office manager, is already settled at her desk when I walk inside. She gets here before I do most mornings to start a pot of coffee and line up the agenda for the day. I may not drink coffee much, but she loves it, as do most of our clients and the guys that work for me when I need the extra help to stay on schedule. I do need to see about hiring someone else, at least part-time, to work alongside me in the bays. We are getting busy enough with the basic touch-ups and regular clients that it's time.

"Can you help me get a job description and roles, and responsibilities built out for a part-time tech to help out? I'd like to get someone in here more consistently once Tilly and I get back from seeing her dad over the holidays. And I don't think you want to be hanging out changing oil and detailing cars," I ask her as I pull my list of appointments. I need to call Clark and see when he wants to come drive the Shelby. His buyer is set to get the car in just a little over a week.

"Will do. That shop owner in Montana wants you to call him back. He got another car that he thinks you may be interested in."

"I do not want to work with him. He wasn't exactly forthcoming with the state of the Charger a few months ago, and I don't want

By the time the weekend rolls around, I am beyond dead tired. One could say, afterlife tired. I know some of it is the stress of everything that is going to be happening next week, and the relief of finishing classes and assignments for the semester. But it's done and I don't have to worry about anything else – at least when it comes to classes. Now I get to fully immerse myself in final preparations for the wedding, prepare myself for when Dad and a few of his associates come out, and then move my things into the house. I have a separate bedroom, and while originally it felt a little weird, it's also just another reason why I know Jonathan was the best choice. He respects me as a person, and while I'm pretty sure he wouldn't mind an actual relationship with me, he isn't pushing for it.

We have five years to figure things out between us, so there's no need to rush. It's enough to try to get a handle on the contracts, Masters Auto Body, and Pink Every Day, plus finishing my classes. I don't need the added pressure of a physical or romantic relationship with Jonathan. If it happens, great. If not, I think I may honestly be bummed. At least I know he's going to be exclusively mine until our fifth wedding anniversary.

I'm enjoying the last few minutes of quiet in my twin bed in my dorm room before Corinne wakes up and the group gets here to help pack up the last things. I would love to host everyone for dinner (or at least for tea) once we settle in fully, but I don't think that's going to happen until after we get home from Chicago. By then, we'll have settled into our new routines and maybe I won't blush every single time Jonathan smiles at me. Speaking of Jonathan...

Jonathan: Hey, pretty girl. I'll be over with the car in about an hour. Do you need any more boxes, totes, or tape? I can grab some things from the office here at the house, or I can swing by the store. Let me know.

Me: Hey, you. I could use another few garbage bags so I can set aside some stuff for donation and then a bag for trash. And maybe some more bubble wrap. I ran out while packing up my books last night. I don't have many left, but they're my special editions and signed books, and I really don't want them getting damaged during the drive or while we get things into the house.

Jonathan: I can do that. Did you sleep well? I know there's probably a lot running through your head right now, but I hope you were able to turn it off long enough to rest.

Me: It was okay. I'm nervous about my dad getting in. I think I'm going to be slightly stressed until we get back home from Chicago.

Jonathan: That makes sense.

Jonathan: I like that though.

Me: What do you like?

Jonathan: That you call our house your home.

Me: You make it feel like home. Even if we aren't living together yet, I like spending time with you, and even though it's not how we would have wanted things if we had chosen everything for ourselves, I'm glad it's with you.

Jonathan: Me too, Tilly.

Jonathan: I'll see you soon. Dress warm, it's cold out here.

Me: There's work to do. I'll get sweaty if I layer up.

Jonathan: I thought I told you that I'm the knight in shining armor. I do the hard and dirty work, and you get to be the "passenger princess."

Me: If you insist.

Jonathan: I absolutely do.

13

- June

- Wednesday

2:00 tail light replacement

185-201

- Week 24

04 46 ☀ 21:10
01 15 **24**

Chapter Twenty-one

JONATHAN

CRANBERRY ORANGE VITAMIN C SMOOTHIE

Social Post: It's moving day. One step closer to saying "I do."
#justlife #coloradocouple #countdowntoweddingday #movingin
#ourchosenfamily

Image Description: Stack of boxes in the living room of the house.

"Is this the box with the pretty books?" I ask Tilly as we begin unloading at the house. She only had a nightstand and a small bookshelf to bring over as far as furniture goes. The rest was her clothes, some photo albums, mementos from college, the few things she brought from Chicago, a whole lot of tea and accessories, and enough romance novels to create a small library. I'm already thinking through a way to add more shelves and displays throughout the house. I already have some things planned for her books, but I'd like to incorporate these as well. I just need to see which of these are for display and which are for reading. I'm

sure she's read most of these at least digitally, but it's obvious she has spent some money on these.

"The ones with the pink glitter tape on the sides, yes. Can we put all the book boxes in the office for now until we can figure out where they are all going? I need to plan out my shelves now I have a little more room." Tilly grabs a duffel from the back of her car, and Sasha, Kylie, Ashley, and Corinne are all here helping with the smaller stuff as well. From what we can tell, the last of the registry items and things from Mr. Chance have arrived, and most of it has been put away already. While Marcus, Matt, Luca, Rowan, and I work to get the last of the furniture assembled and the boxes of books inside.

Kylie created a beautiful reading room and home library for Tilly, and today is the first time she's going to see it. I told her it was my wedding gift to her, so she wouldn't be able to look until we got closer to the big day. I'm saving a section of the shelves for her to organize. After doing a little homework, thank you, Matt, for the social media expertise and a little bit of digging, I found out which books she already has and which ones she would most likely want physical copies, special editions, or secondary copies of. Her personal library of 500 titles is about to get a whole lot bigger. And I can't wait to show it to her. I'm hoping to wait until everyone leaves and then show her before we call it a night.

Between all of us, it doesn't take long to unload everything. Furniture is built, shelves are stocked, and there's a candle burning on the kitchen island countertop that smells like a spiced chai. Tilly has laid out a charcuterie board for everyone to snack on and has three pitchers of different iced teas brewed as well. When she's the one able to set the stage and decide to do it, her hostess skills are spectacular. And it's obvious that she loves it. She lights up when she is doing things for her friends. She's been the one to work alongside the team at Pink Every Day for their receptions, fundraisers, and community projects, too. Sasha may be at the forefront of the organization, but Tilly is happily on the sidelines, making sure everything runs perfectly.

"So, has Jonathan shown you his wedding present yet?" Ashley asks Tilly as she sets out the glasses next to the tea containers. I should probably order some pizzas now that I'm looking around at everyone. It's approaching dinner time, and while the charcuterie tray is amazing, Rowan still definitely eats like a growing teenage boy.

"Not yet. Hopefully, I can convince him that he can show me tonight after you all leave." She throws a wink my way, and I can't help but smile back at her.

"Are you staying here starting tonight? Do we need to wash your bedding or anything like that?" Sasha asks, and I can tell she's trying to tactfully ask if the extra bedroom set up is for show or if that's where she is actually sleeping.

"I was able to wash it all yesterday and then get my room all set before I left. I figured it would be a good transition into being here full time. And the next few days are going to be crazy. We won't get to spend much time together, so it makes sense."

The amount of eye contact that everyone is giving, well, everyone, is moderately comical. They all know that this is more or less a business arrangement. Luca and Matt are the only ones who know I have actual feelings for Tilly. She may suspect I do. I know the other girls think I like her. It doesn't come as a shock that the majority of Tilly's books had a label on the box that said "he falls first." Apparently, it's a pretty popular trope in romance. Looking around the room at those who are coupled up, I have to stifle a laugh. Matt, Marcus, and Luca all fell first in their respective relationships. And with how amazing Tilly Chance is, it's no surprise that I am already so gone for my fiancé.

TILLY

Shortly after everyone leaves the house, I make my way back to the kitchen to wash the dishes and decompress from the day. This place already feels like home. Jonathan feels like my home.

Even though this place was only his for a long time, he's made space for me in every room. We worked together to update the décor, picked out new furniture and necessities, and even worked my music collection into his. He didn't just make room for me, he brought pieces of me and my style into every available opportunity.

We switched the dish soap to one I like. I told him I'm open to trying the eucalyptus in the shower before I ask to take it down. The leaves in the shower definitely surprised me the first time I saw them in there. And the two-car garage now has my car and one of his in it. Yes, one of his. I've found out that he owns four cars – two are practical and two are pretty. That's how I classify them anyway.

"Would you like to see your wedding present tonight, or do you want to wait? I'm not sure how tired you are after what we did today, but I wanted to give you that option." Jonathan comes up next to me as I place the last glass in the drying rack.

"I'd love to see it tonight if it's ready. I've been dying to see what you have been working on for me!" I'm practically jumping up and down from excitement over this. I know it's in one of the rooms upstairs, but I've been so good and haven't peeked in there at all. We head up the stairs together, him walking right behind me. And I'm all too aware his eyes are likely on my hips, my legs...and my butt. I'm proud of my curves, and I haven't missed that Jonathan seems to appreciate them as well.

"Okay, I need you to close your eyes. Good. Now, I'm going to hold your hand and walk you inside. No peeking." The feel of his skin against my own sends heat up my arms, and I find myself thinking back to that night that he held me while I cried. I liked that a lot. Probably more than I should have. It probably would have been even better had it happened on a night that I wasn't crying my heart out. After taking a few steps into the space, Jonathan turns my body a bit so I'm most likely turned toward one of the walls. I don't even remember what was originally in this room, so I'm dying to see what he did with it.

He moves to stand behind me and, after a moment, rests his hands on my shoulders, holding me steady. I wonder if he can feel the excitement I am practically vibrating with right now. "Alright, open your eyes." His permission is practically a prayer on his lips. And when I do as he asks I gasp in shock and surprise. This library is everything I could have possibly dreamed of. Floor-to-ceiling shelves on one wall mostly filled with books, smaller shelves on the second one that are mostly bare, and the third wall has seating options – yes, options. There's a bean bag chair, a recliner, a couch, and a hanging chair, too. And then the fourth wall has an electric fireplace, a ladder with an assortment of blankets hanging on the rungs, and a mini cabinet setup complete with snacks, teas, and water bottles.

"Jonathan, this is incredible. This is...everything. Would you hate it if I just spent my days in here when I don't have work?" I start walking over to one of the shelves, noticing that some of the titles look familiar, but I know I didn't have these before. This entire shelf is all special edition books, from some of my favorite authors. How? Where did these come from? I turn around to look at Jonathan to see him standing in the middle of the room, hands resting in his front pockets, a contented smile on his face.

"I had a little bit of help," his confident tone tells me that this was still mostly him.

"Thank you. I don't even know how to properly convey how thankful I am. This is perfect. And those special editions aren't cheap. You didn't have to do that."

"I know, I wanted to. I found several from a few different companies that I thought you might like. And some were just in line with the color scheme of the shelves. If there are any others I'm missing, let me know. I'm still waiting on the last few S.J. Tilly books from Brightside Candles, and then that's everything I have already ordered." I've been walking toward him while he's been talking about the books, and now I'm standing directly in front of him. Close enough that I have to look up in order to meet his eyes with my own.

"You're amazing. I don't even have words. The fact that you went hunting down some of these editions. Thank you." I have to fight to hold back the tears. Jonathan must notice, though, because he brings his hand up to cup the side of my face, using his thumb to gently stroke my cheek and to brush away a tear I missed. His touch both soothes me and sends a wave of desire through my body that I was not prepared for. He looks at me like I am his everything. And while that absolutely terrifies me, would it be so bad if I lean into those feelings myself?

"You're amazing, Tilly. And if this is something that I can do to show you that you deserve good things, I'll gladly hunt down any pretty book you want." I can tell he wants to say something else, but he's hesitating.

"What is it?"

"I really want to kiss you." The voice inside me starts doing impromptu cheer routines over the thought of this gorgeous man wanting to kiss me, touch me, to show more than friendly affection, but bring it to a romantic level.

"I think I need to tell you something first."

"What is it, sweet girl?" I take a deep breath before sharing something that I've never told anyone, not even Ashley.

"You'd be my first."

He pauses for a moment and just stares into my eyes. His thumb, which had been caressing my cheek, comes down to lightly swipe over my bottom lip. The one I really want to feel pressed up against his own.

"First, what?"

"First, everything." Please, please, please don't think I'm a weirdo for being nearly twenty-two and not having experienced this before.

"I'd be honored to introduce you to all kinds of pleasure, Tilly. And kissing you in the library I made for you – just for you – that seems like the perfect way to end this day." His voice is practically a whisper, a plea. He wants this as badly as I do.

"I think I'd like that." He looks at me again, a silent question in his gaze. And I know he wants a different response. I smile at him, "I know I'd like that. Kiss me, Jonathan."

Jonathan keeps his hand on my face and neck as he bends down to meet his lips with my own. The kiss is tentative and soft, like he's making sure I'm actually okay with this. I find myself drawing closer to his body. The strength and solid build of him feels so good against my curves, and the way he pulls me even closer as he puts his other hand on my waist makes it even better. I know he's trying to be a gentleman, but I need more. More of his kisses, more of his touch, more of him. I know part of it is probably the excitement of all the new things coming, but I can't deny the attraction I feel toward him.

When I push up onto my tiptoes and wrap my hands around his neck, pulling him closer, he takes that as the invitation it is. I open slightly for him and am greeted with his tongue entering my mouth, tangling with my own. It isn't hot and heavy. It's not desperate. It's sweet and gentle, a quiet claiming.

Part of me is amazed I've gone this long without experiencing what it feels like to be kissed, to be touched, to be loved. But the other part is glad that I get to experience this with him. My body responds to his touch like it already knows that I belong to him. It isn't just a kiss, it's an awakening of my entire soul. I don't miss the way I need to press my thighs together to alleviate some of the ache that is now there. Or the way I can feel the hardness behind Jonathan's jeans. I believed him when he said he wanted me, but feeling how much he wants me – it's practically overwhelming.

By the time we separate, I can feel the heat in my cheeks. I let my breaths calm while he holds me close. And when I wish him goodnight, I almost hate that I walk away from my amazing fiancé so I can get ready for bed in my own room. I may not be ready to say that I am fully falling for this man, but I'm getting close.

13

• June

• Wednesday

2:00 tail light replacement

165-201

• Week · 24

☼ 04:46 ☽ 21:10
☾ 01:15 **24**

• July
26 27 28 29 30 01 31
03 04 05 06 07 08 02
10 11 12 13 14 15 09
17 18 19 20 21 22 16
24 25 26 27 28 29 23
31 01 02 03 04 05 30

Chapter Twenty-Two

JONATHAN

BREVE LATTE

Social Post: And she is done. Thankful for no snow on the ground so this beautiful restoration project can be delivered to her new home. #shelby #classiccars #carrestoration #masterscarrestoration #nococars

Image Description: The Shelby all ready to be picked up on the lot in front of Masters Car Restoration.

"We can just send for a car to go get him..." Tilly offers again as I get ready to head to the airport to pick up her dad. She's been nervous all morning, barely finishing the smoothie I set out for her and only picking at the fruit on her plate.

"Tilly, I want to do this. It's okay. It'll give me a chance to talk to him and see if I can figure out how to have some form of relationship, even if it is just a professional one. I can hold my own. And he's probably expecting me to pick him up."

"He isn't a nice man, Jonathan. He has a way of controlling every situation, every conversation. You saw how much he tried to manipulate things while we were in contract negotiations. And that was for his daughter. He is going to be a whole lot less attached to your happiness than mine." Her eyes fall down to her plate as she starts pulling apart the pineapple pieces that I cut up this morning. With how much she's deconstructed her food, it's hard to tell how much she's actually eaten, and I don't like the thought of her not taking care of herself.

I walk over so I can sit next to her on one of the bar stools. My empty smoothie glass sits next to hers, and I have to smile seeing that she finally finished drinking it. "I am on your side with this, Tilly. All of it. I'm your partner, your friend, and soon to be your husband. Know that I have your back. Your dad may be a powerful man, but I'm not scared of him. The contracts are signed, there's no changing that now. Let's focus on the good that's happening this week." Her smile is soft, like she's trying hard not to continue voicing her concerns. I rest my hand on hers until she turns it over so I can lace my fingers through her own.

She smiles up at me in anticipation, and I know she's waiting for the kiss I give her on the back of her hand when I hold her like this. I give it to her and have to hold back the laugh at the spread of the blush on her cheeks. "I trust you to handle whatever he throws at you. Just know he's going to be looking for opportunities to twist what you've said to get what he wants."

"I'll be careful. How are you going to spend your day?"

"I have a library to get familiar with and an afternoon tea appointment with the girls."

"I can't wait to hear all about it. Do you want to meet back here so I can pick you up for our dinner, or do you want to meet me at the restaurant?"

"Would I sound incredible needy if I asked you to come get me?"

"Not at all."

The drive down to the airport is quicker than I would have liked. I have to work to keep the anxiety under control. I've talked to Mr. Chance a few times over the phone, but it's mostly been through his staffers. While part of me wouldn't have minded having one of the guys with me, I know this is going to be an opportunity for him to size me up, see who is marrying his daughter. While I wasn't his first choice, I want to make sure he knows that I am going to be the best choice. And seeing that in five years we will both be financially stable, and hopefully still happily married, just makes it that much better.

Already knowing what some of Tilly's dad's expectations are, I've dressed in a pair of khaki pants and a button-down shirt. I wouldn't be surprised to find that Mr. Chance travels in a full three-piece suit. Once I make eye contact with him in the main luggage pick-up area, I'm actually glad to see he's in just a suit jacket, no tie. He must recognize me from all of the online research he did because he walks right over to me. I extend my hand first to greet him, also subconsciously telling him that I'm not intimidated by his presence. I will respect him as Tilly's dad, but that's about it.

"How was the flight, sir?" I ask as we shake in greeting, and then reach for one of his luggage pieces.

"It was decent. Things were a little bumpy coming into Denver, but that's to be expected with the mountains." We walk side by side toward the parking garage where my vehicle is waiting. At least I brought one of the "pretty cars" as Tilly likes to classify my sports and muscle rides.

"Do you need to stop for coffee or would you like to head to the hotel to rest before dinner tonight?"

"The hotel is fine. Our reservations are at six?"

"Yes, sir. And you have a ride already reserved for that?"

"Yes, thank you for arranging that for me."

The conversation dies there, and I'm thankful for the brief

respite. Because I know it won't last for very long. I was right because we aren't on the highway for more than fifteen minutes before he starts up again.

"I'd like to see your shop if we have the time. Can we make that happen today?"

"Yes, we can definitely do that. I have a few phone calls to make while we are there if that's okay with you. I have a project that is done that I need to call the client on. He has an out-of-state buyer, and I need to make sure it's fully ready for the pickup. With all of the dinners and meetings this week, I need to have it ready to go for him."

"Totally understandable. I'm excited to see what you have been working on. I found a few magazine spreads and online profiles of cars you've had the opportunity to finish. You do a good job, Jonathan. Cars may not be my area of expertise, but I can tell you take pride in the work you do."

"Yes, sir. I've been around cars since I was young. My dad used to tinker around in the garage, and now I get to do that on a more professional level. I have a buddy who does mechanical work, and I do body work. There have been a few times that we have had the opportunity to work together on rebuilds, too. My passion is classic cars, and I got to work on my top wish list vehicle this year. This Shelby is beautiful, and I'm glad you will have the opportunity to see it when we get to the shop. It's scheduled to be picked up later this week."

"I heard about it when I was doing the initial research into you and your company. You may not have been my first choice as a partner for my daughter, but I'm glad she at least picked someone who takes pride in their work and who hasn't thrown talent and money away."

His tone is condescending even if his words aren't.

"I'm good at what I do, Mr. Chance. And your daughter is one of my closest friends. I'm honored that she asked me to be alongside her for the next five years. And I want you to know right now, it's my desire to be by her side until the end of my days. I love your daughter, sir. And if she never fully reciprocates that, I'll be happy knowing that I get to treat her like the queen she is for as long as she allows me to do so."

He doesn't respond to that, and I let myself enjoy the silence. I'm confident in my choices. And he is going to have to accept that I'm not going anywhere. No matter how much money or how many businesses he throws at me. Tilly is my home. And I will gladly spend the rest of my days being hers.

Part of me feels like I should be nervous about bringing Luis into my space, what I've built, and where the majority of my passion and ingenuity goes. He has engineered an empire based on politics and less-than-ethical business deals. I have constructed mine on blood, sweat, passion, and tears. But this is who I am. And I will confidently show him what I have created and attached my name to.

Walking into the lobby, Angel greets us with a smile and an offer for a hot drink. Mr. Chance asks for a black coffee, and I ask for my usual – she knows how I like it. And then I lead him into my office.

Many of the spreads my cars have been featured in are framed on the walls. It's a warm space, designed so I would be happy to come in here to work or to have some quiet in between appointments. There's a couch and a mini fridge, and lots and lots of automotive and classic car books, manuals, and parts company brochures on the shelves. It's not as cozy as Tilly's library, but it's where I can work productively for hours or have consultations with potential buyers, collectors, and clients.

"Do you have any classic cars?" I ask as he peruses the spreads on the wall. I wasn't able to get much information on his car situation from online sources. And none of the other shop owners that I work with have dealt with him before. Yes, I asked around.

"I've had a few off and on. I generally just look for things that I can invest in and then sell to collectors or gift as closing deals are wrapped up. I actually get to pick up another acquisition soon. It was supposed to be a gift to Jason's father at the wedding next month, but now that things have changed, I may just auction it off."

"That would have been a generous gift to close out the contracts. Which car was it, if you don't mind me asking?"

"The Shelby sitting in your garage right now."

I don't respond for a moment, trying to figure out the timelines in my head. This doesn't fully line up. "But I have had that car since August. Clark was able to take ownership of it in June. How did it end up in my garage?"

"I may not be fully present in Tilly's life, but I know who her friends are. And I've been wanting to diversify my investments a little more as I approach my time ending as mayor and in the political sphere. I knew you were one of her friends, and your name has come up many times in the research I did after I purchased the Shelby. I don't agree with a lot that Tilly does, but I wanted to do what I could to check on her without being physically here. One way I can do that is by seeing how her friends and those she associates with handle their money, their clients, and when handling high-cost investments. You did a good job on this. Clark has been sending me updates, and I'm impressed with all that you were able to do, under the original quoted budget."

"I'm not in this to become a millionaire or take advantage of those who trust me with their retirement plans or inheritance. Word of mouth and the trust of my clients are more important to me than making money quickly by being dishonest and cutting corners. Clark has been one of my biggest supporters since I started out on my own. Do you want to see the finished product?"

"I'd love that, but I'll trust you with the keys. You know the roads out here better than I do. And I still haven't decided what I'm doing with it now I'm not working with the Barnes family anymore."

That last statement surprises me a little bit, but I don't push for more information. He wanted a ride, so let's make that happen. "Let me just call Clark first. I'm not saying I don't believe what you have told me, but the car is still in his name, and I need to run this by him."

"I appreciate that you operate with integrity. It's something I wasn't always able to do with being in the political sphere, and some days, I wish I had made different choices with my career. But decisions have been made. And all I can do now is set my daughter up for success and stability to the best of my ability."

"So, why go after what she loves with Pink Every Day? It's such an incredible organization, and you should be proud of what she is doing there. If that company were to be closed down, hundreds of employees, supporters, non-profits, and consumers would be impacted. They may still be a start-up, but their impact is far-reaching. If you really want to set Tilly up for success, why go after that?"

Angel comes in after a subtle knock to bring us our coffees and a small assortment of snacks that we keep in the lobby fridge. Once Angel closes the door behind her, Mr. Chance takes a moment to collect himself and sip on his coffee before responding.

"At the end of the day, I am a businessman and a politician. I want my daughter and my wife back in Chicago. I want her settled in with an established family so she doesn't ever have to go without anything that she may want or need. The Barnes family has that. I know them, and it's a calculated risk that I already know the potential outcomes for. Pink Every Day is new. It's a volatile industry that is rooted in trends and how much husbands allow their wives to spend on cosmetics and things that aren't deemed a 'necessity.' Yes, they are doing good work and giving back to their community, but it's still new. Cosmetics are one of the first things to go when budgets get tight. I didn't want Tilly investing everything into something that can be gone the next time the market drops or one big influencer posts something negative about the company."

I listen to all he's said and take it in. It makes sense from his perspective, but it still feels like an easy out. "Now that you know that she's going to be here, with me, for at least the next five years, how do you see things now?"

"I have a meeting next week with the board of Pink Every Day. They don't know it's with me since I booked the appointment under one of my lesser-known LLCs. I plan to offer to fund their next five years of production, payroll, and product development. I want to set Tilly up for success. And if it's with makeup and skincare, then I'm going to back her on that."

"I think you need to tell her this. She is still operating under the assumption that you don't support her, that you don't recognize her passions. She thinks you see what she does as just a hobby or putting off an actual career for the sake of something else. Hearing that you want to see her succeed and you are investing your money behind that will go a long way in repairing your relationship. I know I'm not a dad yet, and I don't know if I will ever have the opportunity to hold that title. But it's what I see. Tilly is amazing and so good at what she does. Let her know you see that too."

He nods in acknowledgment before sipping his coffee. And then takes another sip. "I'm going to need to order some of this for my offices; this is phenomenal."

"Good things are made right here in Colorado."

Chapter Twenty-Three

TILLY

JASMINE PEARL TEA

Social Post: It's my turn. #weddingdetails #champagneandpearls #teahousewedding #peoniesplease #completelytilly #pinkeverydayco

Image Description: Detail flat lay photo of my wedding shoes, lipstick, and earrings for today.

This week has been both incredibly long and way too short. My dad is here and has seemed like an entirely different person than the man who was in my home while I was growing up. Mom is here too, along with her parents. I thought that Dad may bring out some business associates or some of his office staff, but he left them all at home. When I asked him about it, his response was, "This week is about you, not politics; they don't need to be here." I was even more shocked to find out the reasoning behind buying the Shelby and having Jonathan fix it up for him. It may have been a little messed up, but this is how he was taking care of me and making sure I was alright out here.

I'm still a little wary to see where things continue to go. Is this just him playing nice? Or is he finally deciding that a relationship with his daughter is more important than some status symbol? I'll have to wait and see how this plays out. He actually listened when I told him about the work I'm doing with Pink Every Day and even offered to make some phone calls to some marketing firms he's worked with over the years. I won't be able to manage a full internship, but having resources that I can connect with to ask questions and find out what's currently working in the industry – that is going to be invaluable.

He even came with me to see the Pink Every Day offices and the area that we hope to get a storefront in one day. He mentioned that he has some things he wants to go over with me, but that can wait until after the wedding. Hearing him tell me that he is excited to see where the company goes and that he respects all that Jonathan has built has me seeing Luis Chance in a whole different way. It's so much more than him pushing his agenda on my life. Maybe we can actually pursue a relationship now that we have cleared up some things.

But today is definitely just about Jonathan and me. Even with all the conversations this week, Dad was still adamant that we marry for the originally contracted five years. He wants us to start our lives out with stability, and this will ensure Jonathan and I both have what we need to take those next steps in our businesses. I can't fault him for that. I'd have preferred a bit more say in when all of this was going to happen, since it would have been nice to have graduated before getting married, but I'm glad the wedding day is finally here.

Sasha is doing my makeup, and she surprised me with a custom-made lip kit as her wedding gift. It's such a gorgeous mauve that complements my skin tone perfectly. A coordinating lip liner and lip gloss finish off the package. It even comes in a sparkly pink box with the title "Wedding Ready x Pink Every Day."

"This really is absolutely perfect. I love how you pair things together. We should see about offering a few variations of this for a future collection."

Sasha adds a little more finishing spray to my face and then pulls out her phone to take a few pictures so I can have them later. We opted out of a professional photographer for the getting-ready portion of the day. We will have someone for the ceremony and tea reception afterward, but for this part, we wanted it to be intimate and special just for our friends. She surprises me by turning her phone around to show me a full release mockup that I haven't seen before.

"We have these going through the final stages of testing and development now. Five wedding-ready lip kits as part of our Summer Bride collection. This one is for you, and then we had a set paired for Kylie, Ashley, me, and also one for darker-complexions. So, we each have our perfect lip kit for events moving forward. There are a few perks to being the owner of a beauty brand." She winks at me and I can't stop the laugh in response. I love seeing Sasha so happy and thriving in what she has built.

"That's amazing. Thank you so much! I can't wait to see the full product line so we can start working on the marketing and release campaign."

"That can wait until after the wedding. Today is about you, not Pink Every Day. This is set to release in May, so we have time to work on all of that when you get back from the Chicago trip. Now, let's go get you married."

I never imagined feeling as beautiful as the way Jonathan is making me feel looking at me right now. I may be confident in my body and with my curves, but not many men have ever given me a second glance. And I was okay with that. I lived my life under the assumption that I would find my partner when the time was right. And my weight and curves would be something that he dealt with or tolerated because he loved me. But the way Jonathan looks at me as I walk down the small aisle, surrounded by our friends and family, hearing his nephews whispering about my princess dress, I can clearly see the desire in his eyes. And it feels so good.

I smile up at my fiancé as I stand in front of him, holding a bunch of varying shades of pink peonies in my hands. There are some perks to having a dad with a gross amount of money – out-of-season florals. And these are my favorites. The light scent of the flowers mixed with his cologne, and a little bit of black tea that's brewing behind the counter, fills my entire body with a sense of comfort and home. Yes, we were able to book the day at the tea house. And it's beyond perfect.

Matt is the one officiating, and it feels like a full-circle moment. Our friendship group has become family, and I couldn't imagine anything else to make this day more perfect. The ceremony is simple and sweet. We opted out of the "does anyone object" line because only those who truly know us are here. Matt moves the conversation from the initial greetings and talks of who we are as individuals and how we're preparing to begin our lives together. And then we hear a voice I was not expecting to hear ever again… especially not today.

"So, I don't get any say in this?"

Jason Barnes stands at the door of the tea house, in a suit, his hands on his hips like he is scolding a child, and not interrupting my actual and very real wedding ceremony. Before I can voice anything, Jonathan grasps my hand, giving me a sense of stability, showing me that he is here for me and will back me in however I want to handle this. I'm still debating a response when my dad surprises everyone by standing up and turning to face Jason at the door.

"I'm pretty sure you don't have an invitation, Mr. Barnes. Our relationship is strictly professional, and you have no reason to be in attendance at this event. I will discuss any concerns and questions you have when I return to Chicago. Now, please see yourself out after you apologize to my daughter and the rest of her guests for the rude interruption." And then he sits down and faces forward, as if to fully dismiss Jason and show that Jonathan and I are the center of his focus once again.

Jason doesn't immediately leave, seemingly flustered over the public call-out from my father, but stays at the door, staring at me with a look of hurt and anger. I really don't want this to escalate further, and I don't want this entire day to turn into an opportunity for the men to posture over status and size. I'm about to ask Jonathan to walk him out when Marcus surprises me. Ashley's fiancé stands up, buttons his suit coat, and walks to the back of the space. He leans in to say something to Jason, quiet enough that I can't make it out. All I see is the color draining from Jason's face and then his back as he turns around and leaves the tea house.

"Carry on," Marcus lets us know as he unbuttons his jacket and sits back down next to Ashley. She looks as confused as I feel, and I have to stifle a laugh over the change in events. Marcus is the oldest one in our group and can come across as a grumpy professor sometimes, but I've never seen him intimidate another person before. I know he had confronted Ashley's stalker when that happened, but he doesn't know Jason and had no personal interest in telling him to leave. But I'm thankful he did all the same.

A few minutes later, vows and rings have been exchanged, and I'm waiting (not so patiently) for Jonathan to lean down and kiss me, making it fully official. When he does, I am filled with that electric excitement that ran through me when I first kissed him in the library last week. And I have to force myself to not deepen the interaction. My parents do not need to see me with my tongue down my husband's throat. I can feel the blush spreading across my cheeks at the thought, and Jonathan must be thinking the same because he chuckles against my lips before pulling away.

"Happy wedding day, Mrs. Masters."

"Happy wedding day, husband."

A few hours later, after a special tea reception, Jonathan and I are on our way back home. We opted to stay at our house tonight rather than a hotel. Especially since romantic feelings are just starting to develop, and we haven't gone any further than pretty tame kissing, I didn't want anything to be pressured into happening before we were actually ready. He parks the car in the driveway and then gets out to open my door for me.

He takes my hand and leads me to the front of the house, our house. After unlocking the door and opening it a little bit, he shocks me by picking me up, bridal style, of course.

"Put me down, I'm too heavy," I practically squeal when he starts walking into our home.

"You're not too heavy, Tilly. You're my wife, and I'll happily carry you over the threshold." He places a kiss on my forehead and then puts my feet back down on the floor.

"I've never been a little girl. I'm not used to being picked up and carried around." I try to brush it off so I don't start blushing again or call too much attention to my insecurities, however handled they may have been.

"I like carrying you. And I *can* carry you. I want to. I know this wasn't how we would have planned to start a relationship, but I'll happily show you each and every day that you're the woman I want to do life with. All of you, Tilly."

I don't even know how to respond to that, so I toe off my heels and head up the stairs to my room. I need a moment to see how I feel about this. Sure, I knew he liked me. And yes, I know there's more to those feelings on my side of things too. But does this mean he is wanting to do this past the contracted time? How would that even work? I begin taking off my dress and then realize I'm going to need some help. It may be a cute cocktail dress, but the closure at the base of my neck needs more dexterity than I can give behind my back. Opening the door, I go to call for Jonathan, only to find him standing there waiting.

"Oh, you surprised me." And there's that blush again. "Would you be able to help me?"

"Sure," he steps closer, just inside the doorway to my room. I spin around and move my hair out of the way so he can see the clasp. I feel his fingers on the hook and eye closure, and then feel his lips just above it, placing a soft kiss on my skin, sending shivers down my body. A moment later, the clasp is undone, and the zipper is being lowered. He stops once he gets to my waistline, where the zipper halts, and then rests his hands on my hips. His hands are big, and the weight of them holding me still as he kisses my neck again sends shivers down my entire body. And a heat that I wasn't expecting into my belly begins to grow. Why does this feel so good? I force myself to turn around in his hands so I can look up at him.

"Tell me what you want, Tilly." His command is just over a whisper, but it's filled with a layer of desire that I know matches mine.

"I'm not ready for more right now, but will you kiss me like this is our real wedding night?"

"Tilly," he pauses, waiting for my eyes to meet his own again. "Yes?"

"This *is* our real wedding night. You are my wife. I am your husband. And I will gladly kiss you every single time you ask and however often you allow my lips to caress your skin. I am yours, Tilly Masters. And I love you."

I'm not able to come up with a coherent response to what he just said, because his lips are on mine and I have to force my legs not to buckle with the growing desire. I have to hold back a moan of pleasure as he presses my body against his. The feeling of his body up against mine is the perfect mix of strength and gentleness. I feel safe in his arms. But I also feel wanted, needed.

"Tilly, you are the most beautiful woman I have ever seen." Jonathan's eyes trail down my body as my dress falls to the floor. I'm in front of him in just my white lacy bustier and matching lace underwear. I have never felt as desired as I do in this moment. The bustier pushes my ample cleavage up even more than normal, and Jonathan wastes no time coming back to my lips and then trailing his kisses down my neck to my chest to the tops of my breasts. The sensation of his stubble on my skin sends a shiver of need through my entire body. And I don't realize it until after I've done it that my fingers are in his hair, holding his lips to my chest, not wanting him to stop yet. It feels too good.

"Jonathan," I breathe out his name, needing more but not knowing what to ask for. He stops his exploration with his mouth as he makes eye contact with me again.

"Do you want me to stop, pretty girl?" It takes me a moment, but then I realize that we probably shouldn't be doing this. This is way too fast to be making things physical between us. I can't deny the attraction on my end, and I know he feels it too, but it's just too much right now. We are both breathing heavy, even just from the kisses, and I see the moment he realizes I'm not ready for more. He doesn't make me feel bad about it, he just leans in to place a gentle kiss on my lips and then my forehead.

"Sleep well, Tilly. I'll have breakfast ready for you in the morning. Let me know if you need anything." And with that, he adjusts his pants a bit and then turns around and leaves my bedroom.

I flop down rather ungracefully on my bed. This is a problem. I think I'm falling in love with my husband.

13

• June

• Wednesday

2:00 *tail light replacement*

165·201

• Week · 24

☀ 04:46 ☀ 21:10
☽ 01:15 · **24**

• July
26 27 28 29 30 1 2
3 4 5 6 7 8 9
10 11 12 13 14 15 16
17 18 19 20 21 22 23
24 25 26 27 28 29 30
31 1 2 3 4 5 6

Chapter Twenty-Four

JONATHAN

CINNAMON ROLL BREAKFAST SMOOTHIE

Social Post: Road trip prep is happening as we get ready to go to Chicago for our wedding reception with Tilly's family. Now to decide which of these smoothies I'll be freezing and which ones we are taking with us. #smoothies #greenjuices #mealprepping #roadtripping

Image Description: Variety of smoothie containers, fruits, veggies, and other ingredients on the counter that need to be cleaned up and put away after an afternoon of preparing base smoothies for the next few weeks.

Taking care of Tilly has become my favorite way to spend the day. Our bubble of being home and just getting to know each other is about to be over, though. We had the option to fly to Chicago, and when I asked Tilly if she would be open to a road trip, she agreed. This may be one of the only times we have the flexibility and space to do it. There's definitely some risk of weather, but we don't for sure have to be back home until Tilly's birthday. At least this time we know it's going to be a few days each way, and we have a car that shouldn't overheat.

"Are you a 'pack all the snacks before we leave' kind of road tripper or 'stop at the gas station for snacks' kind of road tripper?" Tilly asks as she zips up her luggage. Her mom bought us each a new set as her wedding present, and I'm glad we have the opportunity to use them so soon. Tilly's is pink and mine is a slate blue color, and they surprisingly look really nice next to each other.

"I'm good either way. I'd like to pack a small cooler so we have options in case we get stranded on the road or in between stops. I can go to the store for your favorites today while you run into the office." Sasha mentioned, when we had her and Matt over for dinner last night, that she got some skincare samples in and wants Tilly to try them out for a few days. I think she wants me to try them out too since they're doing a 'skincare for everyone' campaign in the fall. That was something I wasn't aware of in the cosmetic industry – they have to plan ahead so far because of production, marketing, and distribution. They're already planning out their launches for the following year. And the way it all fits together is pretty incredible.

"Sounds good. I'll make a list of things I think I need. Is that alright?"

"Absolutely, love. We are going to take three days to get to Chicago and then four days back with the planned route. And we are in Chicago for a week, right?"

"Yes," she adds another sweatshirt to her suitcase before closing that one as well. "We have the reception that my dad is hosting, then we have the surprise I planned for you, and then a few days to just spend time together." She ticks off her mental list, and I know she is going through her color-coordinated calendar as she does.

"When do I get to know what my surprise is?" I ask, knowing I have some for her too, for this trip and for when we get back home, but I have to give her a hard time about what she has planned for me. What she could have set up in such a short time definitely has me curious, but her dad holds a lot of influence in Chicago, so it's not terribly surprising.

"When we get there. Now, shoo. I need to get some work done before I head to the office." She makes a shooing motion with her hands, and I reluctantly comply.

"Text me with your favorites or things you absolutely hate that I need to avoid. I'll see you back here for dinner?"

"Yep, I'm cooking tonight. I'll be home by four." I turn to leave and then think better of it, so I walk back into the room and place a kiss on her temple. I love this woman so much already, and I can't wait to see where our relationship grows now that she is giving this thing between us a chance. But in the meantime, I'll remind her that I'm here and that I'm wholly and irrevocably hers.

By the time I get home that afternoon, I have a full cooler bag full of snacks for the trip and then a few other things I saw that reminded me of my amazing wife. Yes, I'm fully aware that I'm being sappy, and no, I do not care to change that. Have you seen her? I am still absolutely in awe over the fact that I get to call her mine, at least for the next five years. And I'm going to do everything in my power to turn that into the rest of our lives.

"Do you need help with anything, or are you good?" Tilly calls from the kitchen as I step inside the house. I make my way toward her so I can put the cold food away before I bring the other bags to the bedrooms.

"It smells amazing in here. What are you making?" I place a quick kiss on her forehead as she stirs something in the pot on the stove before I start unpacking the bag's contents onto the island countertop.

"Some comfort food. I know we leave tomorrow, so leftovers will have to get put in the freezer, but I really wanted chicken soup."

"Well, it smells incredible. I'm excited to have some. I'm going to run upstairs to put this stuff with my luggage, and then I'll be down. Did you think of anything else you may need, or are you good to go?"

"I'm all good. Ready to head out tomorrow with you. I just need to plug in my Kindle so it's fully charged before we leave." And that reminds me that I need to grab the new books I bought for her and put them in my bag. I've learned that most authors release books on Tuesdays, which is a small reason why we are leaving on Wednesday. I wanted to run to the bookstore to get a few new books that I knew she had been wanting to read.

"I can do that for you when I head up if you'd like; that way, it isn't forgotten."

"That would be amazing. This is just about done, so don't be up there too long." She points the wooden spoon at me that she's been using in a mock chastising tone, and I don't even try to stifle the laugh at her antics.

"Yes, ma'am." I give her a little salute and then hurry up the stairs. And get a nice surprise when I pull open her drawer where I know she keeps her Kindle. I was expecting to find her reader and maybe a few other bookish things. I was definitely not expecting any toys of the vibrating variety. And now I'm going to have to fight through dinner with thoughts of her using said vibrator and trying to play off the fact that I saw it. I debate for a moment before I grab it from the drawer and then go to my own room to pack it away for the trip. I may see about doing some of my own playing and surprises, too.

"Good morning, love. Are you ready to go?" I let Tilly sleep in this morning since I know she doesn't rest great at hotels. I had to force myself to get her up now because she looked so comfortable sleeping in her bed. I'm already crossing my fingers that she'll come join me in mine – our bed – when we get home from this trip.

"Yeah, I just need twenty minutes if that's okay? I want to take a quick shower and then get dressed." Her sleepy smile up at me is one of contentment and of a good night's sleep.

"That's perfect. I have your smoothie for you downstairs, and your bags are in the car. We don't have any reservations until our hotel tonight, and that can be adjusted." Her stretching out in the bed has my eyes gazing over her body. The way her shirt rides up, revealing just a slice of her soft, creamy skin beneath. And she doesn't miss my stare because her nipples harden under her

T-shirt, which I recognize as one of my own. I don't even apologize for looking or give her a hard time for snagging one of my shirts. I wonder when she grabbed that. I may not be allowed to touch, yet, but she is beautiful and I want her to know that she is desired and wanted.

"I'll be down soon. Do I get something special if I guess what you put in my smoothie?"

"Anything you want," I send a wink her way and then close her door behind me. By the time she comes downstairs, I have the cooler packed with juice containers, grilled chicken wraps, and some of our favorite teas that I cold-brewed overnight. Tilly has been liking acai bowls some mornings for breakfast, so I've been staring at my containers in the fridge for the last ten minutes trying to figure out if there's any way I can take it with us without making a mess or throwing the majority of it away.

"I think we can just plan to have those when we get back. Can they go in the freezer?"

"I don't think so. I'll have Alayne come by to raid the fridge once we leave. The boys are apparently eating everything in the house now that they are home on Christmas break."

"Sounds good. Can we have them over for dinner when we get back? I'd like to get to know your family better, and the boys seem to adore you."

"What's not to love?" Tilly grabs the kitchen towel and snaps it at me, having me jump out of the way to avoid her attack.

"Yes, I know you're amazing. That's not the question I was asking." She blushes again, and although part of me wants to push it a bit, tease her a little more, I don't want her to ever think that I'm coming after her or questioning what she's saying.

"We can do that. I like seeing you play hostess. Now get your stuff so we can be on our way. It's supposed to snow tonight, and I'd like to be at our hotel before the storm hits, just in case."

"I need to see if I can figure out my smoothie first!"

I pause to wait for her guess. It's a little game we started playing this week, and although she usually gets one or two ingredients right, she has yet to get a full combination right. I don't make it easy on her, though, and it's fun to see how long I'll be able to stump her on these.

"Is it a strawberry banana fruit base with spinach and the B vitamin boost?"

"So close – I went with a probiotic boost this morning."

The first three hours of the drive were pretty straightforward. Highways and minimal construction traffic luckily meant that we made good time. And after a quick lunch and a stop at a tea shop we found on the main street by the restaurant, we are on our way again.

"The storm is set to hit town around eight, and we're on track to get to our hotel at six. So, we should be okay on that front. I'm just a little worried about rush hour traffic as we get closer to the city."

"At least we don't have to worry about Hans overheating on this trip."

"Hans? Did you name another one of my cars, Mrs. Masters?"

"Yes, I did. This one felt like a Hans. What do you think?"

"I'm guessing it's another character from one of S.J. Tilly's books?"

"Yep."

"Do I want to know some of the reasons why you bring up this book boyfriend? Do I have something to be worried about?"

"I know this is still new, but I think you're my favorite book boyfriend. Hans is a close second, though." The combined laughter in the car brings me a sense of joy, and the way she interlocks her fingers with mine and waits for me to kiss the back of her hand brings a sense of home that I've come to associate with my wife.

At the hotel, I've a gut feeling that we may be here a little longer than planned. The sky is turning dark a lot faster than I was expecting, and I'd hate for us to be holed up inside without food or comfy clothes or things to do. Tilly is inside, checking us in at the counter, so I stack my duffel on top of her rolling bag and then grab the cooler and my backpack. This should keep us good to go for as long as we need it. And I have to smirk knowing what is hiding in the pouch of my backpack…if the opportunity presents itself for some play time anyway.

"And just to let you folks know, we'll be watching the weather. The storm is expected to hit us within the next few hours. We have backup generators ready and additional water if needed." The receptionist is going over the details with Tilly as I join her.

"What do we need to do if we need to spend another evening here?" I ask as I look over the paperwork the receptionist handed over, going over the amenities at the hotel. If we weren't traveling during prime winter storm weather, I'd have looked into Air BNBs or Bed and Breakfast-type establishments. But I wanted the stability and options that came with chain hotels this time around.

"Just call down and let us know. Ideally, before check out, if possible, so we know how many rooms need to be switched over or can be booked out tomorrow night."

"Will do, thank you." Tilly is polite with the woman behind the counter and then turns to me, seeing all of the bags and her extra coat draped on my arm as well. "Do you think we need to stay an extra night?" She whispers as we head to the elevator bank just past the main lobby.

"I don't know for sure, but I want to be prepared just in case. I wouldn't be surprised if we end up needing to. We planned for this, and we have time. No stress, love," I lean down to kiss the top of her head once we get into the elevator.

"I love that I don't have to worry about those things with you. You think of all the contingencies and possibilities. And you take really good care of those around you. I know it's just who you are, but I appreciate it. I appreciate you, Jonathan."

And now I'm the one blushing.

Chapter Twenty-Five

TILLY

PINK FLAMINGO FRUIT TEA

Social Post: Travelling to the Midwest during Winter is always a little bit of a risk. I guess if we get snowed in, I'll at least have some new books to read. #bookish #whatimreading #newbooks #snowedin

Image Description: Stack of new books and my Kindle on the bed, open blinds show snow falling in the background.

I don't sleep great in hotels. And I don't do fabulously on car rides. But for some reason, I found myself saying yes to Jonathan when he brought up the idea to road trip out to Chicago. At least we'll be able to take our time with this. And I have to laugh when I open the hotel room door.

"One bed again?" Jonathan asks even before he sees the space.

"Did you do this on purpose?" I tease him as I bring my overnight bag into the bathroom, pulling the skincare from Sasha, my own toiletries, and makeup out to lay on the counter.

"Tonight? Yes. Tomorrow? No. It was a King bed at this hotel or two twin beds at the one-star hotel down the road. The hotels were fairly well booked out here for this week."

"That makes sense. Thank you for making that call. This is perfect."

"Dinner will be here in about forty minutes. Figured we could order in for tonight and then play tomorrow by ear. Do you want to change, or do you need to get any work done tonight?"

"Nope. I get to be fully off while we are traveling and in Chicago. All I need to do is try out the new skincare products and get a few pictures of that, maybe some videos. But the different hotels are going to be perfect for this, so I can get a variety of content."

Jonathan smiles at me before beginning to pull out his own items that he'll need in the bathroom. And I have to laugh to myself again as he lays out his skincare items. He's the first guy that I've met that actually has a full morning AND evening skincare routine. And we've had more than one evening where we are side by side at the bathroom vanity exfoliating and masking together.

"So, does that make this a business expense?"

"I think so." Maybe? Finances and accounting are not my area of expertise, and I'm kind of looking forward to getting to hand things over to Jonathan's tax pro in a few weeks. There are definitely some perks to being married to a guy who already has his finances in order and is happy to take care of me in every way.

After a light dinner of grilled chicken, Caesar salad, and a tomato and basil soup, Jonathan puts a movie on the TV while I set up in the bathroom. I need to test out the new skincare and shoot some content while I'm at it. I have a few different tank tops and hair wraps to wear, so that way, each morning and evening that I use the products, I have different neutral backdrops for the content. I never know how the campaign will end up being set up for a product launch, so I try to get a good variety of base content that I can edit and play around with.

Thirty minutes of testing and recording later, I'm ready to call it a night. I don't want this entire trip to turn into a marketing opportunity. Plus, I only have sample sizes of the new product line, so there's only so much I'll be able to do with this. After cleaning up the counter and putting the products away, I head back into the bedroom to see how Jonathan's doing. And I realize a moment too late that I'm just in a silky black tank and short pajama set, without a bra. I changed in the bathroom after finishing recording, thinking I'd start settling down for bed. And forgot that I'm sharing a room, and a bed, with my husband tonight. And I don't think he hates the idea of that very much, by the way he's looking at me as I stand in the doorway.

"I can change into something else if you aren't comfortable with this. I kind of totally spaced that we are sharing a room tonight. I'm sorry."

"Don't apologize, Tilly. You're gorgeous, and I love every opportunity I get to see more of you." And the blush is back. This time, I know it's spreading down my neck and chest, which is clearly seen above the low cut of my tank top. All the cleavage on display. Awesome.

"You keep saying things like that and I'm going to start believing you." He doesn't bother to correct me. I know he means what he says. I'm still coming to grips with the fact that he believes the words he says though. I may love my body, but I've never had any man look at me the way my husband does.

"Do you want to come lie down with me?" He pulls the blankets back next to him, showing some very soft sheets and a stack of pillows that I have to hold back the desire to jump into. I grab the hair tie from my wrist and tie my hair up in a quick bun on top of my head, then walk over to the bed.

My husband is very comfortably lounging on the side closest to the door, in a pair of low-slung black sweatpants and no shirt. Of course, he's not wearing a shirt. Looking that good, I don't blame him. After plugging my phone into the charger, I snuggle down into the bed, pulling the covers over my lap and then reaching over to grab my Kindle off the nightstand. Jonathan's phone rings just as I'm about to dive into my newest book about an older mountain man. I wonder if there are any snowed-in scenes in this one...

"Totally understand," Jonathan answers the person on the other end of the line, and is then quiet for another moment before answering what must have been a question.

"Yes, we'll plan to stay here. I'll call down if we need anything else, but we should be okay. Just let us know once things are settled and we are fully dug out, and we'll hopefully be able to continue on our way the day after tomorrow. Thank you for letting me know." He hangs up the phone and then looks over at me.

"Looks like we get to stay warm and cozy in this room a little longer. They're already calling for those traveling to stay put and keep the roads clear overnight as the plows work to keep up with the storm."

"Well, if I have to be snowed in with anyone, I guess my husband is as good an option as any." I joke with him and he doesn't hesitate reaching over to tickle me in retaliation after he places my Kindle back on the nightstand, of course.

After nearly making me pee my pants from laughing so hard, Jonathan lets up, but not until he's partially straddling me on the bed, holding my hands down so I wouldn't tickle him back. And I'm sure that the heat in his eyes mirrors my own.

"Can you do me a favor?" I tentatively ask, second-guessing the words even as they pass my lips.

"Anything."

"Kiss me?" And he does without any hesitation, like he was just waiting for me to give him the green light.

The way his lips devour mine, claiming, taking, pouring his want and desire into every motion, the way his hands hold my own, and the way his hips are pinning me down. It's not a hard pressure, just enough to show me that he is in charge right now, and he wants this – by the looks of it, more than I do, and I've never felt so needy as I am in this moment. I have to pull away from his kisses so I can catch my breath. He doesn't stop though, trailing his lips to my chin and then down my neck.

"Is this okay?" he asks as his breath settles on the space where my neck meets my shoulder, adding a soft bite to his trail of kisses.

My response is a gasp at the surprise, and the way his hands grip just a bit tighter, "Yes. I like your lips on me like that." I can't get any more words out because I'm not able to think clearly enough to come up with sentences anymore. His hands move to my wrists and then down my arms, tracing, caressing, leaving a trail of electricity everywhere he touches.

"This doesn't have to go any farther than this, Tilly. I want you, and I'm not going to pretend that I don't. But I want you to want this too. Tell me what you want, love. Whatever you want, I'll do it." The way he's holding my gaze has a full-body shiver running through me. The fire in his eyes is unlike anything I've ever seen. I never thought I'd have someone be this viscerally attracted to me. Curves and stretch marks and belly jiggles and all.

"Um, I've never actually done this...so yeah, I don't know exactly what I want." So many emotions travel through my husband's eyes, and I don't know how to describe them. Desire is evident, surprise, and maybe a bit of excitement too. I think he likes the idea that no one has ever touched me this way before. I told him this in the library before when we shared our first kiss, but I think he's fully recognizing it now. He's been my first kiss, my first make-out session, and I think I want him to be my first everything. Maybe even my only everything.

"Will you tell me if you don't like something or you're getting overwhelmed?" I nod and he continues, "Will you tell me to stop if you need a pause or if you want to be done for tonight?" I nod again. "Will you let me make you feel good, Tilly?" I begin to nod, but he stops me. "I need to hear your words. Tell me what you want, love."

"I want you to touch me, make me feel good. Please." As his lips descend to my neck again, that spot that lights a fire inside me, I let myself fall into the sensations his hands and lips give me. I almost miss the whispered words as he exhales next to my ear.

"How do you make yourself feel good? Will you show me?"

"I don't..." I trail off, not sure how to answer that. What is he asking?

I find out what he means by that as he reaches under his pillow and pulls out a small silicone toy – my small silicone toy.

"Where did you?" I don't finish my question because he's turned it on and is lightly tracing over my nipples through my tank top. Oh, that feels way too good. I gasp at the sensation, squeezing my eyes shut, not wanting to see what Jonathan is staring at as he plays with my body underneath him. I know I'm probably not his first, but I want to just revel in the moments of him figuring out what my body likes, what I like.

"Do you like that, pretty girl?" His voice is husky and filled with need, and I don't miss the way he shifts to relieve some of the pressure on his growing length in his sweatpants.

"Yes, why does that feel so good?"

He just chuckles his response before leaning down and sucking the nipple not currently being played with from the vibrator into his mouth. I arch into his touch, gasping at the differing sensations.

"Oh, Jonathan, don't stop, please don't stop." He adjusts his position again, just a bit, so he's better braced on top of me, but he doesn't stop. Not until my tank is sufficiently wet from his mouth.

"Is that how you use this?" He shows me my toy again, and I know I'm red from a mixture of embarrassment and pleasure. I shake my head in response, hoping he doesn't push me to use words.

"Do you want me to keep trying to figure out how you like to use this, or do you want to show me?"

I must find another burst of confidence because even I'm shocked at the words that come out of my lips. But I think I'm ready to show him that I may be ready to take this further too.

"I'll show you what I like if you do the same."

His jaw drops, as surprised by my request as I am. "Do you want to watch me taking care of myself while you do the same?"

I nod, but he stops me again. "Words, Tilly."

"I want to watch you stroke yourself, making yourself feel good, and I'll use my toy to show you what I like."

"Can I add one request to that?"

"Yes."

"I want to see you. I'll take off my pants if that's what you'd like, but I'd love to see you do the same. I want to see how wet you are for me, pretty girl."

I'm moving to comply before he even finishes his request. Not letting myself feel nervous about baring myself to him, because I want to see him too. I want to feel his eyes on my skin as I take in the strength of his thighs, the muscular V that leads to what he's revealed now that he's pushed down his pants and underwear.

I may have very little experience with pleasuring myself, and I have no clue what to do with pleasuring a partner, but the way he draws his hand up and down his length is absolutely mesmerizing. He's able to fist himself and shows me in his movements what he likes, what feels good. I'm about to ask if he can help me do it too, wanting to bring him pleasure, when he reminds me what I'm supposed to be doing.

"Show me how wet you are, Tilly. Lie back and spread your legs for me. I want to watch as you make yourself feel good, as you coat your fingers and that toy in your desire. Show me." His voice is husky and heavy with need, and I don't even attempt to answer with words. I just prop myself up on my elbow and use my other hand to slide through my sex, marveling at how wet I already am for him.

"Do you like watching your husband, Tilly? I can tell you want to come and touch me, but you have to finish what we started first. Grab that toy, turn it on, and show me what you like." His hands grip himself a little tighter, and I realize he's trying to not finish yet. He wants to wait for me. As soon as the vibrating silicone touches my clit, my head falls back on a gasp. I am so incredibly turned on right now.

"This isn't going to take long. Oh, that feels so good." My voice is breathy, and I can't believe I just told him that.

"Imagine it's my fingers on you, Tilly. I'm the one making you feel good. I'm the one bringing you pleasure. It's your husband between your legs, touching, teasing, needing you." I close my eyes and do just that, thinking of his hands on me, wondering what his mouth would feel like; would the stretch of his dick hurt, or would it feel incredible?

"Jonathan, I want to see you. Please. Come with me, I'm so close." Who is this person that's taken over my body? I am not a dirty talker. And I know this is pretty tame comparatively, but I want him. I want to make my husband feel the ecstasy that I'm on the edge of feeling.

"Don't stop, Tilly. Keep going. Let me see you shatter for me. I'm close too. Let me see you drench that toy and your fingers in your pleasure."

With a few movements and a groan from my husband, I find my own release. I don't let myself sit with the embarrassment or questioning of what we just did. I wanted this. So did he.

"I need to get cleaned up. And then I'd like to come back to bed. Is that okay with you?" His question is cautious, probably knowing how much I'm holding back the desire to run away and hide.

"I'd like that. Don't be too long."

"Never. If I have an invitation to share our bed, you won't be able to distract me for very long from lying next to you. And especially now that I've seen what you look like when you come..." He trails off, and I don't miss the heat in his eyes. "You won't be able to keep me away from you. I'm going to take every opportunity you give me to make you feel good, Mrs. Masters."

"I think I'm going to hold you to that, husband."

I didn't think being snowed in for an extra day would be all that exciting, but we ended up enjoying our time together with some card games, an Ocean's movie marathon, and a new book from Jonathan. Apparently, he ran to the bookstore before we left since it was Tuesday and a bunch of books I've been waiting on had been released. Gotta love a man that pays attention to the little things.

Leaving the hotel, it's beyond freezing outside, and I'm again thankful that Jonathan has a car with heated seats. Because we lost a day of travel with the snowstorm, we're trying to make it a little farther than we originally planned on our way to Chicago. We're still going to be able to split it between two days, but we'll only have four hours to go tomorrow if we get as far as we hope tonight. At least Jonathan knows now that I'm not the best road trip companion. He made me such a cozy space to nap in while he drives. And when I wake up, we are pulling into town where we are staying for the evening. And I can honestly say I'm disappointed when we get into the room and see two queen-size beds.

A hot shower, more content recorded, and Friends re-runs on

the TV make for a quiet evening. And I try to focus on the rest we both need, wondering why I don't just ask Jonathan if I can sleep with him. Because after last night, I think I prefer sleeping in his arms to being by myself.

"Tilly?"

"Yeah?"

"There's enough room if you want to come sleep over here. I'll keep my hands to myself if you want, but I don't think I can sleep unless you're snuggled in with me."

I don't even wait for him to finish talking before I'm crawling into bed with him.

"This dress looks so stunning on you! I'm glad you decided to bring it with you so we can have another special day for you here with your father's friends and business associates." My mom finishes with the clasp on my dress and adjusts one of my bobby pins, holding my hair in place. We're having the reception at the Country Club – I know, original – and I waited to change until we got here. There's plenty of snow on the ground and I didn't want to chance slipping on the ice in my heels and getting my dress all dirty. Most girls only get the opportunity to wear their wedding dresses once, and already I've had two chances to get all dressed up in my pretty princess dress.

"How many people did Dad invite to this thing?" I touch up my lipstick and then put it back in my pocket. Yes, my dress has pockets.

"The guest list with RSVPs is at ninety. The catering staff is handling everything, so we can just enjoy some champagne and mingle. I don't foresee anyone else coming that wasn't on the list. We closed down the Club for the night." Mom gives me another once-over and then opens the door to Jonathan waiting on the other side, in his suit, looking like a million bucks.

13

- June

- Wednesday

2:00 *tail light replacement*

185 201

- Week 24

- July

Chapter Twenty-Six

JONATHAN

PEACH BLUEBERRY SMOOTHIE

Social Post: Part one of our trip is done. Ready to show off my beautiful bride again tonight. #sappypost #completelytilly #receptiontime

Image Description: Photo of Tilly putting on her earrings for the reception tonight. Thanks to her mom for sending me the amazing behind the scenes shot of her.

The last few days have been incredible. Being able to have Tilly all to myself, getting to know her has been even better. And being able to have those moments where she lets me see the other side of her – the side that's open to exploration, to pleasure, to being my wife – that has been incredible beyond words.

As I wait for her to finish getting dressed for the reception tonight, I can't help but mentally go through all the things that I would love to do if we had an endless amount of time to drive back to Colorado. She may not be the most alert road trip companion, but she makes it a lot easier to drive those long distances. And having her in my bed each night is definitely an added perk.

Seeing Tilly in her wedding dress the first time was a vision. This second time, now that I know a bit more about how she looks under the undergarments she wears under the pretty white cocktail dress, is jaw-dropping.

"You look amazing, Mrs. Masters. Are you ready to do this?" I hold out my arm for her and she takes it without hesitation.

"Let's do this." She smiles up at me. I give her face a brief once-over, making sure it's a genuine response and that she isn't hiding from this. She had a really good talk with her dad while he was out for the wedding, and I hope he will honor the way he wants to parent moving forward that he told her during that meeting between the two of them. It would break my heart to have her expect one thing and be given another from him.

I must not be hiding my apprehension as well as I originally thought, because she pulls me down a little so she can whisper in my ear, "Control what you can and leave the rest." I nod and place a kiss on her forehead. She knows exactly what I need to hear, and knowing that she is reminding herself of the same thing helps me take it fully to heart.

We follow Tilly's mom to the main party space – a gorgeous room with floor-to-ceiling windows overlooking a white winter wonderland. It's probably a rose garden or outdoor dining area when it isn't covered in snow, but it adds to the fairytale setting that my bride mentioned she would love to see. The tables are covered in a navy-blue base tablecloth and then topped with a shimmery off-white fabric. Some of them have sparkling centerpieces while others have peony floral arrangements. I know she doesn't need expensive things or to be lavished with high society events and gifts, but seeing the way she appreciates every little thing brings a warmth to my chest. Her dad gave her everything she could have asked for in planning this reception. And in this moment, it's enough.

Luis Chance lets us take it all in before he comes over to greet us. Tilly gets a kiss on the cheek, as does his own wife. I receive one of those strong handshakes that politicians give in order to show their importance and status while still trying to come across as a relatable businessman. I haven't talked to Mr. Chance since he arranged for the Shelby to be picked up at the shop. He decided he wanted to keep it for himself – after I told him I'd strongly suggest he store it for the winter months. I don't need all my work to be undone after one winter of snow and ice-treated roads. That stuff eats through the underside of cars so fast. And repair costs add up fast.

"Glad you made it in okay. How is the hotel?" He asks me as Tilly twirls around the space, looking at all the little details with her mom. Guests should be arriving within the next thirty minutes, and we will be announced in just like at a traditional wedding reception, so now is the chance for her to fully take it all in.

"It's perfect, thank you for the upgrade, sir." I'd booked a King suite room at the Hilton not far from Tilly's childhood home, but Mr. Chance knows how to use those connections and they bumped us up to a premium suite. It'll be perfect for those extra days that we are spending here so we can prepare small meals and unpack a bit. While I don't mind living out of a suitcase for a few days, my wife prefers to unpack so she can fully get ready every day. And I love being able to give her that. Seeing her matching shoes under each planned outfit hanging in the hotel closet brought me a sense of joy and rightness I wasn't expecting. It's the little things that make her the beautiful person that she is. And I am honored to get to call her mine.

"It wasn't a problem at all. I wanted to see if you were interested in going to an auction with me next week. I was able to get an invitation for two, and I'd love your expertise and opinion before I make a purchase. I'd like to get another vehicle for you to potentially restore for my wife now that she's home and maybe another one if it catches your eye. These cars are an investment, and I value your input. And I know I'm not supposed to tell you this, but this is your surprise from Tilly. She's excited to give you a chance to see some other cars. When I told her I had an auction to attend, she practically begged me to find a second ticket for you to attend as well."

"I'd love that. Let me know details on when everything is happening and I'll coordinate with Tilly. I know she wanted to pack up a few other things from the house. I'm not sure if there's anything else on her agenda though. Thanks for thinking of me and for valuing my thoughts on cars, not just to attend this with you, but to help you pick out some cars to purchase. I love what I get to do, and it means a lot to me that you recognize that."

"You put in incredible work on the Shelby, Jonathan. And I heard about what happened with the Montana car from Tilly. You operate with integrity and value the vehicles that are entrusted into your care. It shows that you have a stable business plan and understand that it's more than a quick sale with the cars that are given to you. I appreciate that as a businessman and as a father. And, I know I didn't say this before, but thank you for encouraging me to talk through some of my concerns and plans with Tilly. You helped us repair that relationship, and while we still have a ways to go, it's a start. I need you to know that I truly am thankful for you."

I nod in acknowledgment of what he said. More words aren't needed. It's his way of saying that while I may not have been his first choice for a life partner for Tilly, he's happy that this is how things have settled with us.

An hour later, I'm twirling Tilly around the dance floor, her cheeks flushed from laughter and maybe one too many glasses of champagne. "You look like a princess, my sweet girl." There are so many people here, and I only know my wife's parents, but at least no one is treating my girl poorly or questioning her decisions. From what I've been able to overhear, people are excited about the company she has a position in running and have been eager to see the cars that I've worked on. Mr. Chance even brought a few magazines that feature work I've done, and one that did a spread on Pink Every Day last October.

"I feel like a princess. I don't want this level of attention on any kind of normal basis. But this is amazing. Are you having a good time?" She catches her breath as we walk back toward our table, ready to sit for a little while and have our first course now the waitstaff has begun preparing for the meal.

"I am. Seeing everyone gush over you and what you are doing

now in Colorado is amazing. I love that they are excited for you. I wasn't sure what to expect with this group, knowing that many of them are in politics or lobbyist companies. They could either be upset that you weren't marrying into the Barnes family or completely apathetic toward it and be attending today just as a social gathering with free champagne." Tilly laughs a little at my last observation, and I reach over to lace my fingers with hers before giving her soft skin a kiss. "But I'm glad that they are invested in what you're telling them about the company. And I'm pleasantly surprised that your dad is in a kind of 'proud grandpa' mode with the magazine spreads for both of us." He really is kind of cute, showing off all the pictures in the magazines like he would be if it were a grandchild and not a car or lipstick.

"And did you see that Mom has our last October collaboration collection with her? She has one of each of the products and got some of the material from the websites printed out on nice brochure paper, and is passing it out. I've heard more than one person ask when they can buy stock in the company." Her chuckle is one of 'can you believe this!!' levels of excitement, and I lean in to place a quick kiss on her lips.

"Everyone else is just now realizing how incredible I already know my wife is."

"It sounds like you have had a few fun conversations too. What's this I hear about car shopping with my dad?" I don't miss the teasing tone in her voice, absolutely giving away that she planned this well before tonight. I decide to humor her a bit, not sure how much her dad told her about the auction process.

"I'm pretty sure you already know all this, but it's an auction, so not quite normal car shopping. It'll be a space with a lot of high-end, antique, and sought-after cars with buyers who have the money to back it. I should have a list of cars and starting bids Monday, and then the auction is Wednesday morning. It sounds like your dad wants to get at least one new car for me to work on."

"Be careful, or he's going to keep you too busy to spend time with your new bride." She boops me on the nose as she gives me the admonishment.

"Never. Not even another Shelby will keep me from coming

home to you every night." I take a quick pause before adding something to my statement. "I promise to come home to you every night in time for dinner unless we've made other plans prior. And I promise to hold you close in bed each night, unless you tell me to keep my hands to myself. And I promise to have a smoothie or juice for you each morning as long as you help me when it's time to go tea shopping."

"I think I like that better than your vows from the wedding."

"So does that mean you accept?"

"Does that mean you want me in your bed when we get back home?"

"Nope. I want you in *our* bed." I lean in to kiss her again.

"I like the sound of that." And she kisses me back.

13

• June

• Wednesday

2:00 tail light replacement

185-201

• Week · 24

Chapter Twenty-Seven

JONATHAN

WINTER CITRUS SPRITZ MOCKTAIL

Social Post: I got to attend my first high end vehicle auction tonight with my wife and her father. Seeing these cars and being able to give input on what Mayor Chance should invest in was an incredible experience. And, it ended up raising some much-needed funding for Pink Every Day. #carauction #classiccars #pinkeveryday

Image Description: Program for the auction from tonight along with my notes from one of the cars.

W hat Luis Chance neglected to tell me when he brought up the auction was that he was the one hosting it. And it's not just a normal car auction. It's a charity auction. Each car sold today will have the funds split. Half of the final accepted bid will go to the seller, the other half will go to one of the charities, non-profits, or startups that Pink Every Day has partnered with since they started. Tilly is here with me in a cute twirly black skirt and pink top that matches her lipstick perfectly. And when we walked into the space and saw all of the signage for the fundraiser, the tears in her eyes were instant. After sending up a silent prayer that she wouldn't mess up her makeup and then be self-conscious for the rest of the day, I gripped her hand and led her to our seats while we waited for things to begin.

"Dad, when did you get all of this set up?" Tilly asks as we get settled next to him at a table toward the front of the room. It's a banquet hall, not much unlike the Country Club space we were at just a few days ago. The cars that are up for auction are on poster boards attached to display easels around the room. Twenty cars. Bidding starting at thirty-five thousand dollars at the lowest for two of the models and going all the way up to one hundred grand for four of them.

"I had some time to work on things once I got home from the wedding. I've been pulling away from working with the Barnes' corporation and a few other partnerships that are no longer serving my goals. I was wrong in how I went about trying to get you home, and I'm sorry for that. I can't fix all that I did leading up to today, but I can change how I handle things moving forward. This is something I can do to help with what you love, what you're building. And if you decide to come home in a few years, I want to leave the door open for that to happen."

"I appreciate all of this so much, Dad. But I need you to know that I'm happy where I am. We'll see where things go, but my home is in Colorado now." Tilly squeezes my hand on top of the table, making eye contact with me before she continues, "My home is with my husband."

TILLY

I was expecting to come home with a few boxes of childhood

memories, a new set of China from my grandmother, and maybe some other gifts from friends of my parents that were received at the reception. I was not expecting to have five checks in my purse. One for Pink Every Day and then four others made out to different organizations in northern Colorado that we've had a chance to partner with over the last two years. Between the five of them, they total just shy of half a million dollars. I can't even begin to imagine all the good that we can do with that money.

And then Dad upped the shock factor even more by writing out a check to fund the production, marketing, and distribution of our new skincare line this upcoming summer, with a request to let him know if we ended up needing more money once we started production. And yes, that's on top of what he is doing alongside the other board members and investors over the next five years. His only stipulation was that we include some marketing materials for "men with mature skin" with the campaign. I gave him a set of the samples when he was out for the wedding. He fell in love with the products, and he wanted to make sure that his friends knew they were for them as well. It was actually kind of cute. Shocking, but cute.

"Part of me isn't ready to go back to routines and school. It's been nice living in this little bubble of snow days and road trips with you for a while." I confess to Jonathan as we sit in the driveway of our home. The car is still running, so I'm nice and warm. The snow is falling outside, and I'm not looking forward to unloading the car and then tackling all the laundry from the trip. I wonder if I can sign us up for a laundry service and call it a birthday present to myself...

Jonathan's hand on mine draws me out of my thoughts, and I smile up at him. My husband really is pretty incredible. "I know what you mean. We have some time before classes start up again for your last semester, and then I have a job I need to start around the same time. We have a little bit longer to enjoy our newlywed bubble we've created. Let's just tackle this one day at a time and see where things go from there." He places a gentle kiss on the back of my hand and then gets out of the car, leaving it running so I can stay warm while he goes to unlock the house and garage.

An hour later, I am showered and in comfy clothes, and everything from the trip is at least inside the house. I'll worry about sorting and putting things away tomorrow. Tonight, I want to enjoy being home. I throw my hair up in a messy bun, not bothering to dry it all the way, as I make my way to the kitchen, where Jonathan is making something on the stove. It smells incredible in here. And seeing my husband standing next to the stove, sweatpants hanging low on his hips, hair still a little damp from his own shower – I can definitely get used to this.

"Whatcha making?" My tone is playful as I come up beside him, trying to peek inside the pot that's simmering. I'm greeted with a smile and a kiss on my forehead before he responds to my question.

"My own version of chicken soup. It's snowing, so it felt like soup weather. And Alayne left what I would need to make things in the fridge. You look comfy." I don't miss the way his eyes heat as he trails them over my body. I have never felt so desired, so sexy, as when he looks at me like that. And whether it's me in my wedding dress or comfy jammies, this is how he looks at me. Every time.

"I am. There's something about showering in your own home that just feels so much better. Even though we stayed at some amazing places while we were gone, this is home." I wrap my arms around his waist and just enjoy the closeness while he stirs the soup a bit more. I can get used to this.

After dinner, we're sitting on the couch, watching a movie that I honestly haven't been paying attention to – I have my Kindle and new books released today, I barely realized that the TV was even on.

"Can I brush your hair?" The question is tentative, but there's want behind his words.

"Do you want to?"

"Yeah. That way, you can keep reading, and I can do something with my hands. I feel like I should be doing something even though we just got home and are still technically on vacation."

"I get that." I laugh and then jump up to go get my brush and a few hair ties. I'm not sure what he plans on doing besides brushing my hair, but I don't want to have to get up again. I expected to sit on the floor in front of Jonathan when I got back, but he's brought over one of the foot rests that's actually big enough for both of us to sit comfortably on, and set it in front of him. He scoots to the end of his seat so when I sit, I'm just a bit lower than he is – the perfect height for him to brush my hair. I wince a bit when I take down the hair tie, I must have gotten some of my hair wrapped around it when I put it up earlier.

I don't get long to think about it, though, because Jonathan starts gently pulling sections of my hair apart, and then begins brushing. He starts at the bottom, going slowly to avoid the tangles, and brushing through until there aren't any pulls. I don't know when I give up trying to read the words in front of me because his touch his way too distracting, in a good way. It's soothing and electric all at the same time. When he finishes, he draws my hair over my shoulder so it's in front of my body, baring my neck to him. Before I can ask if he wants me to move, I feel his lips on my skin. Gentle, soft caresses.

"How do you always know what to do to make me feel so good?"

"I don't...but I'm enjoying learning what my wife likes."

I hum a response, because all I can focus on is the feel of his lips on my neck. The way it sends a jolt of electricity down my entire body while also making me an actual puddle should be studied. I find myself arching a little into his kisses while I let my head fall back on his shoulder.

"Are you up for trying something new tonight?" I almost miss his words because, again, focusing on his lips is taking all my attention right now.

"Maybe, what were you thinking?"

"I want to take you to bed and see what else there is that you like, where I can touch you that brings you pleasure. What areas of your gorgeous body like my lips or perhaps prefer my fingers? Where you desire a light touch over a claiming one. I want to learn everything about you, Mrs. Masters." I listen to his words, having to force myself to comprehend everything he's saying to me. After I am pretty sure he's done talking, I turn around enough to make eye contact.

"Take me to bed, husband." And then I'm being picked up in his arms and carried off to his bedroom, his lips on my own the entire way there. As soon as I register that I'm falling, my body hits the bed underneath me. And my giggles of surprise are swallowed by my husband's lips on mine. His body spread over me, pinning me in place in a way that brings comfort and ownership, but not fear, has me aching for even more.

Before I realize what I'm doing, my hands rove over his naked chest, feeling the firm planes of muscle. In response, I feel his hands on my waist, just under my shirt, caressing the skin. He waits a moment, probably seeing if I'm going to tell him to stop, before slowly peeling it off and over my head. I'm sure my hair is fanned out all over the bed and a lot of the detangling work he just did is being undone, but I don't have it in me to care. The heat in Jonathan's eyes as he rakes them over my naked torso has me practically on fire.

"Do you know how absolutely beautiful you are, my love?" I can only shake my head in response because the conviction in his words tells me that he believes what he just said with every fiber of his being.

"Show me," I am finally able to get out because the need coursing through my body is very new and very loud. And I know he's the only one who is going to be able to sate it. He's the only one I want to satisfy it with.

"Tell me if you need me to stop, Tilly. But I would love to explore, find out what you like, what your body craves."

"I need you, Jonathan. I think I'm ready." His eyes meet mine, understanding my meaning but also needing me to say it so he's sure to know.

"Tell me what you need, love. Please." His gaze doesn't fall away from my own. He waits with hopefulness and need in his entire person, but I know if I tell him I need to wait, he'll be okay with that as well. This man loves who I am as an individual, not just my body or the title I hold as his wife. But he wants my body. He craves it just as much as I want his.

"I want you to make love to me, husband."

"Gladly."

Chapter Twenty-Eight

TILLY

SUNSHINE PEACH BLACK TEA

Social Post: We are home!! #coloradocouple #backhome #winterday

Image Description: Luggage sitting on the floor just inside the entryway of our home.

I can already see his hardening length behind the material of his sweatpants. And the need that is growing inside me, the want, the desire, is more than I was prepared for. I want him. I want this. I want us. I have to force myself not to reach for his waistband and pull them down, exposing his desire for me. I want to let him explore, to find out what I like, what my body needs in response to his own. And he doesn't make me wait long.

My gorgeous husband climbs onto the bed over the top of me, bracing his weight on his forearms as our chests brush against each other. My breasts heave behind my bralette, aching to feel his touch. He starts by kissing my lips and then moving down my neck.

The warmth of his mouth through the lace covering my nipples is an incredible sensation. I wasn't expecting to like it, but I do. He sucks and teases before moving over to the other side, and I shamelessly arch into his touch.

"Find something you like?" he teases as he chuckles against my skin and the dampening fabric he's currently playing with.

"Yes, I don't know if it's the material or the lace or just the way you're toying with me, but yes, I like it very much." My response is practically a pant, all while he continues his exploration.

I start sitting up a little bit, needing to be closer. He must realize what I'm after, because he reaches and helps me pull out of the bralette. My nipples are red and swollen from the attention.

"You're so beautiful, Tilly. I love that I get to show you that, to worship this incredible body." His hands caress my heavy breasts before bringing his head down again. I let out an audible gasp when his tongue draws alongside the skin inside his mouth, like he's sucking on my nipple while he's also caressing me with it.

"Oh, I like that a lot," I can't help the giggle when he does it again because it feels so absolutely amazing. He does it a few more times before he moves to my other breast, giving it just as much attention. My body tells him what I'm needing next before I find the words to, bringing my hips up and trying to make contact with something, anything. And then I practically whine when I don't get it.

"I've got you, pretty girl. I know what you need." And then his hands are on my waistband, sliding underneath until he can peel the layers from my body. And I don't even feel self-conscious when I'm lying bare beneath him. He's still in his sweatpants, although his length is doing its best to break through the fabric.

"That does not look comfortable." I go to stroke him through the material, needing to touch him, to relieve the ache that is for sure taking some of his attention. Instead, he laces our fingers before anchoring my hand to the mattress above my head.

"It's my turn to make you feel good, Mrs. Masters. I'll get to that in a moment, but first, there's something I've been wanting to explore for longer than you probably know." I'm not sure why I like the way he has my hands pinned, the way he's so entirely focused on my pleasure.

"And what have you been wanting to do, husband?" I try to sound playful, but I'm sure it comes out more desperate than that. I need something. And I need it now.

"I want to know what it feels like to have your hands in my hair and your thighs around my head as I bring you to orgasm with just my tongue." And before I can come up with a coherent response, my legs are over his shoulders, and his mouth is on my core. He's right. My hands immediately go to his hair, needing to hold him somewhere and unable to reach anything else.

My body acts without my permission, almost bucking up into his mouth, needing more. His exploration is a mix of kisses and licks, finding where I'm most responsive.

"You really...don't need...to do that...oh, Jonathan, that feels so good, what are you doing?" My statements come out as thoughts, and it takes me several breaths to get out what I'm trying to say. But he's not deterred.

"I want to do this. I need to do this. Because you are lying on our bed, open and wet and needy, and I need to take care of you. Let me take care of you, my love." Well, how can I say no to that? How can I say anything to that? The answer is I can't, because his mouth is back on me, and then he's discovering what I do when he drives it inside my entrance. And while I know I want more, this feels so good, too.

"I'm close. Jonathan, I'm so close." I breathe out, not knowing what's going to happen if he's still down there when I come. He adjusts, just a bit, until he can reach up and cup one of my breasts, caressing for a moment, before he's kneading at the ample tissue and pinching my nipple – as he sucks on my clit – and I shatter for him. I don't know if I say anything or if I make any noise at all, because all I can focus on is the pleasure, and the way he keeps his touch steady until I'm coming down from it.

When I can finally see again, he's propped up above me, his lips glistening with my arousal, his pupils dilated, showing his own desire. "How would you feel if that's how I want to start my mornings moving forward?" He smirks at me, and I just laugh. I'm thankful that he broke some of the tension that was growing inside me, the thoughts that I might have done something wrong. Almost like he knows me well enough to know that I would be over-analyzing that entire interaction as soon as he stopped pleasuring me. And man, does this man know what he's doing in that department.

"Can I please have your cock inside me now?" And yes, I do whine that. Because that's what I want, and I'm learning to ask for what I want and not just wait until things are offered. And yes, I want to have sex with my husband.

"Is that what you want?"

"It's what I need."

JONATHAN

"That is so hot, beautiful." I stand just long enough to drop my pants to the floor next to her clothes. And the sight is erotic and comforting all in one. It's the sight of a couple who are comfortable with each other while still not wanting to waste the time to place clothing on a chair or hamper, just drop it on the floor right where we were, and get into bed together. I pull a condom from the side table and set it on the bed.

"I apologize for how quick this is going to be. I know as soon as I get inside you, I won't be able to hold out long." I lean down to kiss her again, and have to hum in surprise when she's the one to deepen it, tasting her pleasure on my lips and in my stubble along my chin.

"That's okay. I have a feeling we'll be doing this again." She smiles up at me and then traces her finger from my lips to her own, and then draws an invisible line down her neck, in between her breasts, over her stomach, and down to her center. And she shocks me when she starts seeking out her own pleasure, dipping her finger inside just enough to tease, before taking it back out again and making sure her clit and area surrounding her entrance are wet and ready for me. I let her play for another moment before I gently take her wrist and slide her fingers into my mouth. God, she tastes so good. She inhales sharply as I suck on her fingers, and I know she's surprised by my actions. I'm glad I'm her first. Because I get to show her how much she is worthy – in my bed and in my life as well.

I reach down and place my fingers where hers were. I know I'm going to need to prep her a little before she's ready to take my dick. I'm not huge, but I'm bigger than her fingers and the toy she's been playing with. She gasps as I slide a finger inside, letting her get used to it before I begin moving a little. Sliding in and out just enough to get her used to the motion and being filled. And then I add another, feeling her stretch around me just as she arches into the touch a little bit more.

"Do you like feeling me explore you, my love?" My voice is husky and heavy with desire. I can't wait to be inside her.

"Yes, oh, that feels good." I chuckle as she lets her head fall back, just enjoying the sensations of my fingers stroking inside her channel. Her nipples are still so hard, and I can't help but lean down to suck on one of them again, just to be given a stronger grip around my fingers as I do.

"We can check that off as something you like too."

"Are you keeping a list?" She seems partly mortified and the other half impressed with the thought. I don't answer, just adjust my hand a bit so I can find that spot inside her that I know will drive her crazy, as I press down on her clit with my thumb. And within moments, I have her coming again. Feeling her grip down on my fingers just has me aching to be inside her so I can feel the same thing around my cock.

"There we go." My words are almost a prayer on my lips, and the way her body responds to me is incredible. As she comes down from her second orgasm, I can tell her body is as ready as I'll be able to get her. Part of me wants to continue worshipping her all night, but I know we both need some sleep. I ease my fingers out, smiling at the evidence of her release along my skin.

I take the condom out of the packet and slide it on before

making eye contact with her. "Ready?"

She nods. And I lean down to kiss her, focusing as much of my attention on her lips as I can and not the feel of her wet heat letting me inside. Even with the condom, I can feel how wet she is, how much her body is ready for me. I go slow, knowing that I need to take this easy, allowing her body to adjust.

"Let me know if you need me to slow down. I promise to make this feel good for you. Focus on me, that's it. Eyes on me, my love." I keep whispering to her as I kiss down her neck, up to her ear, down her jaw, and back to her lips. Showering her with praise and love and everything that I can give her. She is mine, my heart, my love, my wife – and I am so incredibly and completely hers.

After a moment, I'm able to fully seat myself inside her, and we both let out a breath as we just feel the closeness of coming together as one.

"There you are," she whispers up at me, and I smile and drop a quick kiss on her nose.

"You feel amazing, gripping me so tight." I can't even finish my thoughts because she's reaching up to place her palm on my neck and draw my lips down to hers. Our bodies are slick with sweat and desire, and I begin to move slowly, rotating my hips in small circles, feeling around her, finding what she likes, all while she explores my mouth and moans her pleasure into my lips.

My fingers find her nipple and then trail down to her clit. I'm not going to last long, and I need her to come again. Either with me or as close to together as we can. I can feel her tensing around me, urging me in further, and I happily oblige her body's request. It feels like seconds later, but I can't stop the surge as I find my release, feeling her fall over the edge moments after me.

After a few breaths, I pull out slowly, being as gentle as possible, but still noticing the slight wince on my wife's face. Placing a gentle kiss on her forehead, I walk to the ensuite to clean up and dispose of the condom before returning to her side with a warm, wet washcloth.

"That was amazing," she whispers to me as I make sure to get the residual oils from the condom and the small amount of blood, evidence of her first time, off her skin. Climbing into bed next to my sated wife, I wrap my arms around her, holding her body close to mine. Her curves fill up my hands perfectly, and I love the feel of her body against me.

"Good night, my love." I kiss her temple and am surprised by how fast sleep claims me.

TILLY

Jonathan falls asleep almost instantly after settling behind me, cooling down from the sweat that began to form while he worshipped every inch of me like it was his job and his passion all in one. And as I drift off to join him in a very well-deserved rest, I can't help but think of something we didn't plan on when we drew up the contract and planned the wedding.

"I wasn't supposed to fall in love with my husband."

Chapter Twenty-Nine

TILLY

TURMERIC GINGER IMMUNITY BOOSTER

Social Post: In case you also didn't know this – turmeric stains.
#smoothiemaking #kitchenmesses #reallifethings

Image Description: The absolute mess that is my countertop after attempting to make smoothies by myself this morning.

Over the next few weeks, we fall into another sense of routine and familiarity. Most of my things stay in the other bedroom, but I spend my evenings falling asleep in Jonathan's arms and my mornings being woken up by his kisses, not always on my cheeks. That man acts like he needs me as much as he needs sleep, food, and sunshine. I'm not complaining at all, I'm just surprised. Learning about each other as people as well as lovers has become more enjoyable than I could have imagined. I still have no idea what cars are parked in the garage, but I do know his favorite smoothies and why. And with school back in session,

I'm learning what his nephews like as well.

An early morning in February, when I wake up before Jonathan, has me wondering what is going on that feels different. I'm never awake first. I look at my phone to check the time to confirm it's when we normally get up, and that's when I realize that Jonathan isn't looking so great. I rest my hand on his forehead and then place a quick kiss there. The fever doesn't seem too high yet, but he definitely needs a day off. When I shower and get dressed, and he still hasn't stirred, I make the decision for him that he's staying home.

I grab his phone to get Angel's number so I can let her know, and smile when I see the picture he has as his screensaver. It's one from a morning here at the house, me sitting at the kitchen island, products and makeup brushes scattered around me, as I work on content and some email campaigns. It's a moment where I was in my element and happily doing what I'm good at. I didn't even realize he had taken the photo, but then I think about all the moments where I snap ones of him for my own personal smile memories throughout the day when I can't be with him.

Angel has everything handled for today – luckily, nothing is high on Jonathan's schedule, so he has the space to stay home. Now, I have to figure out some smoothies before the boys get here. This could be interesting.

An hour later, I've had a bunch of fresh ingredients delivered so I can make an immune support smoothie for me and the boys and a recovery one for Jonathan. The kitchen is a bit of a mess as I've tried a few different methods of chopping and adding said ingredients to the blender. The boys thought it was quite funny, and I had to laugh too, when I tried putting an entire lemon and three inches worth of ginger in the blender. That did not go well. Now, they're helping me clean up as I pour batch number five into glasses and containers. It's not as good as what Jonathan makes – but I'm not mad at it.

"When do we need to leave here in order to get you guys to school on time?" I ask them as I rinse out the last failed attempt out of a glass before placing it into the dishwasher.

"In about ten minutes. We have some time," Shane replies as he finishes throwing ginger peel into a small bag and then putting it in the freezer.

"Why are we saving that?" I point to the freezer, not really sure why we are keeping that. It's pretty gross as it is, found that out the hard way.

"Uncle Jonathan uses it sometimes for broth or other juices that call for it." Shane shrugs like I should already know this.

"And he has something he does to make it edible, so you can ask him what you did wrong with it when he gets up," Henry adds in a very sweet and helpful voice. Nice.

"Okay, you boys, finish getting your things together. I'll tackle the rest of the cleaning when I get back from dropping you off. I just need to grab a pair of socks, and we can be on our way." They nod in acknowledgment, and I hurry off to the extra bedroom where all my clothes still live to find a thick pair that will be comfortable under my boots. And then I walk across the hall to the room I've been sharing with Jonathan. He's still completely passed out, and I have to push the worry down that's starting to creep up a bit. It's a cold, he'll be fine. He just needs a day to rest and give his body time to do what it knows it needs.

I leave a quick note on his nightstand and turn his phone to silent. His sister and office manager know he's taking a sick day, so he should have no reason to get a phone call outside of the two of them. And I'm not going to be gone long. I've already decided that I'll be taking a sick day from my own classes. It's early enough in the semester that it won't affect much, and I'll be able to be here in case he needs anything. Plus, it'll give me a chance to get all my assignments and due dates into my planner alongside what I'm doing for Pink Every Day.

After getting in the wrong drop-off line, having to call Alayne so she can call the school office to explain why the boys are literally two minutes late, and then getting stuck behind an accident on the way home, I'm ready to crawl back into bed and sleep the rest of the morning away. I'll deal with the rest of the mess in the kitchen after a nap. But when I walk in the house, Jonathan is up, moving around the kitchen, tidying up.

"You're supposed to be in bed," I practically scold him as I toe off my shoes and drop my keys and purse onto the side table by the front door. I hurry over to him so I can check his temperature again and find out why he's not still sleeping.

"Clark called about a potential project."

"But I silenced your phone."

"I know, and I appreciate that. When someone calls me three times within ten minutes, it overrides that. He kept thinking of other things to add to his voicemail, so he kept calling back."

I groan. Out loud. Totally unladylike, but I do. And he laughs at my response before he starts coughing like he's sick – because he is.

"You need to get back in bed. I'll take care of this. Did you find the smoothie I left for you in the fridge?" I grab hold of his hand like he always does with me and start leading him into the bedroom. Maybe I should have him take a shower first while I swap out the sheets. I'm sure he'll sleep better on clean bedding.

"I did. Thank you. I can't really taste anything right now, but I'm sure it was fabulous. Thank you for doing that for me. Did the boys get to school alright?"

"For the most part. Why do they have two drop-off lanes, but they are separated so you can't move to the other one when you realize you got in the wrong lane when you were still on the actual street?" I'm still annoyed about that.

"It's not the best system for new drivers, but it works well once you know what you're doing. I'm sorry you had to deal with that. I'll just shower and then take a little nap, and then I'll get up and head to work for a bit."

"Nope."

"No?"

"We are taking a day off together. I have some computer work to do, and you have some rest to catch up on. And I think I deserve a nap after the morning I had, too. Go shower, and I'll get our bed ready, and then we can both get some rest."

"That actually sounds amazing."

"And then maybe, when I get up, I can work on moving some things around in your closet so I can bring my things in here with yours?" I've been thinking about it for weeks, but now I really want to just be in here with him. And it feels like moving my stuff into his closet and adjusting the space so it fits for both of us is the next step toward being his wife fully, not just because a marriage certificate and a contract say it's what we are.

"I'd really like that. But maybe let's wait to move your dresser into here until I can turn my head without getting dizzy." He smiles at me, and I have to chuckle in response. Sick and still making me laugh. This man really is my perfect partner.

Over the next few weeks, I make it my mission to wake up before Jonathan on the weekends and on Wednesdays. I practice making smoothies, get dinner going in the crockpot, or at least prepped in the fridge, and look over stuff for active Pink Every Day campaigns before the day starts. We both try to clock out from work stuff over the weekends as best as we can, and this way, I can have twenty minutes of intentional work time before we officially start our day. I haven't broken a blender yet, and we've only had to toss one more of my smoothie creations, so I'm calling that a win. Jonathan is still better at making smoothies, but I like that I'm figuring it out, too. Thankfully, I didn't have to take the boys to school again – that was not a fun time the first time around, and I'm still slightly overwhelmed by that entire experience.

"Happy anniversary, Mrs. Master," I'm greeted with a kiss on my temple and a slight squeeze on my hip as Jonathan walks past me this morning. He grabs his smoothie glass and takes a sip as I turn around to face him, waiting for the verdict on how it is. I actually went a bit rogue for the first time this morning and didn't fully follow a recipe. So I'm holding my breath at how he'll take it this morning.

"Okay, this may be my favorite one you've done so far," he smiles at me over his glass after a few more sips. And yes, I do a little happy dance in response, only to have him respond with a full belly laugh. I love making this man smile.

"I'm so glad you like it. I played around a bit this morning and was pretty proud of it." I know I'm blushing from smiling so much, but I am proud of myself. I'm starting to figure this thing out.

"It's amazing. So, how do you feel about getting dressed up and going out to a nice dinner with me tonight?"

"I think I'd love a date night with my husband. Is this a cocktail dress kind of dinner or something else?"

"Cocktail dress – and probably a sweater or light jacket. We'll have to walk a block or two to the restaurant from where we park. Reservations are at five, so you have the whole day to read or we can do something here at the house, up to you."

"Yay, I'm excited. I think that means I have time for a book and a bubble bath." And I don't miss the audible groan from my husband as I make my way to the bathroom, knowing that I'm about to be comfortable and naked and covered in bubbles, and the tub isn't big enough for both of us. Incentive for the remodel list, I keep reminding him.

13

• June

• Wednesday

2:00 tail light replacement

185-201

• Week · 24

Chapter Thirty

JONATHAN

SUNSHINE VALENCIA BLACK TEA

Social Post: Date night with this beautiful lady tonight. #coloradocouples #anniversarydinner #alldressedup #completelytilly

Image Description: Selfie of Tilly kissing me on the cheek as we head to the restaurant for dinner.

I t's our three-month wedding anniversary tonight, and I cannot wait to take my beautiful wife out for dinner. I also have a special surprise once we arrive at the restaurant. The comfort and ease with which we have fallen into routines together have been amazing. I thought I enjoyed being in Tilly's company before, but as I've gotten to know her better, to see more of who she is and what she loves, I realized pretty quickly that I want more than five years with this woman.

But now I'm sitting in our bedroom (yes, it's ours now, not just mine) on our bed, knowing that she is just on the other side of

the bathroom door, naked, in the tub. And I'm trying really hard to be good here and let her have her quiet time. I need something to do that isn't just sitting in there with her while she's reading and soaking. So, I start making some phone calls to keep myself occupied.

Before I know it, she's coming out of the bathroom, all wrapped up in her towel, face flushed from the steam of the shower she took to rinse off afterward.

"What's that look for?" she asks, and I realize I've been staring for longer than what's probably considered appropriate.

"I just have an incredibly beautiful wife. I enjoy looking at her. Is that okay with you?"

"Only if I get kisses out of it," she smiles at me as she walks to stand between my legs, looking down at me sitting on the edge of the bed. Her hair is still wet, and it creates droplets moving down her skin and under the towel covering her body.

"You can always get kisses out of me," I smile practically innocently at her before I wrap my hands around her waist and pull her down – first on top of me and then rolling over so I'm on top of her. And I'm not disappointed at all when her towel opens.

"We have time before we need to get ready for dinner, right?"

"Of course, pretty girl." And then I make good use of the time we have before I need to let her go to put her clothes back on.

Dinner tonight is going to be at an intimate restaurant that just recently opened. It has a classic steakhouse feel, but is elegant at the same time. I'm not sure how to classify it, but they get good reviews, and they were more than happy to accommodate my request for the evening. And my wife looks amazing in her black cocktail dress. It has almost a sheer pink overlay over the black fabric underneath, and the shimmer on the top fabric gives it such a fun look. And of course, she has pink heels and lipstick to match. I went with a pair of dark grey slacks and a light blue button-down shirt, and finished off my look with a black sports coat. And I'm glad I didn't go with the restaurant that required ties.

"So, have we been here before, or is this a new one?" she asks as she puts her arm through mine and we begin walking to the restaurant. The one downside of downtown restaurants is that there is rarely parking right in front of the place unless we go for lunch on a Wednesday. Any other time, we have a little bit of walking to do. Luckily, it isn't too cold, even for the end of February, so the pink pea coat she's wearing should keep her warm until we get inside.

When we get to the door and the host is about to open it for us, I reach for her hand, placing a kiss on my favorite spot to let her know I'm here for her.

"You like surprises, right?" I tease her a bit.

"Usually...why?"

"Just remember that I love you, okay?" She nods at me tentatively, and then we walk through the open door.

I'm sure you already guessed it, but all of our friends and family are just inside, all dressed up and waiting for us. A few yell surprise and greetings, but Tilly just turns to look at me once she takes it all in, excitement and apprehension mixing in her gaze.

"What's going on, Jonathan?" she whispers to me, and I answer by holding her hand and then dropping down to one knee in front of her.

TILLY

Walking into the restaurant, I kind of knew something was about to happen. I wasn't expecting to see literally everyone here, though. Our friends, their partners, Angel, our parents, Alayne and her husband, and yes, even the boys are here. The room is set up like a normal restaurant, but the tables have been pushed together, banquet style, rather than being all separated. And we must have rented out the place because there's no one else here besides the waitstaff, from what I can see.

I spin around and look up at my husband, my excited and nervous husband. "What's going on, Jonathan?" He squeezes my hand and then lowers himself to one knee in front of me. What the heck is going on right now?

"Tilly Masters, a few years ago, I saw you for the first time. And the way you lit up a room, the way you just so effortlessly found your people to connect with, I was absolutely enthralled. A few months ago, I got to start calling you my friend, and then quickly, my best friend. You were the one that I wanted to talk to first thing in the morning and share all my life with, no matter how small the detail might have been. Whether it was a new smoothie recipe I tried or a new pretty car, as you like to call them, that I got in the shop. I wanted to share it with you.

"Then, you asked me to become your partner for the next five years. You asked if I would stand by you as your husband, your partner, your friend. And I happily said yes. I wanted to do life with you and all the little things that I had been wanting to share with you. But now, on our third month wedding anniversary – yes, I do pay attention (he says as an almost aside to the crowd), I want to amend our agreement. I've talked to your dad and to the lawyers, and now I just need to ask you. Will you dissolve our previous contracted arrangement? And will you be my wife, fully and completely? Will you marry me again, Tilly Masters?"

I take a moment to take in his words, the emotion, and the sincerity behind them. I look up to my dad, knowing that I believe what Jonathan has said, but still needing to see that Dad actually has agreed to cancel the contract because I can't let Sasha lose everything that we have built together over the last four years. It's not just my job on the line; it's her passion and the livelihoods of so many people. My dad nods at me, and then I look to Sasha, who does the same. She may have found out about what was in the original contract, so I want to be sure she knows what this could mean if this isn't actually true. But it is.

"I'd love to be your wife, no contract needed." And with that,

Jonathan is standing up and places a gorgeous band on my finger next to my original engagement ring. Adding to the stack and showing the new meaning with the new ring added.

"So then, I have one more question for you." He leans in so I'm the only one hearing him now.

"Yes, husband?" I smile at him again.

"Would you like to get re-married?"

"When were you thinking?"

"How does right now sound?"

Moments later, we are standing in front of friends and family, with Matt officiating for us again. We go through the vows and the ceremony, holding hands, and I giggle like an actual schoolgirl this time around. And when it gets to the part where I say my vows, I amend them a little bit, since we aren't under contract anymore.

"And, Tilly, do you take this man to be your lawfully wedded husband?"

"I love you, Jonathan Masters. And yes, I do, again."

Chapter Thirty-One

TILLY

SPARKLING PEACH ICED TEA
Social Post: Another milestone checked off the list! #graduation #csugrad #collegegrad #officiallyanadult #completelytilly
Image Description: Graduation cap flatlay next to my pink heels.

The days leading up to graduation pass by in a blur. I get to enjoy being a wife and a senior in college. We've also gotten the final packaging in for the skincare launch, and we are preparing for the marketing shoot for the end of May. I don't have to worry about the models or photographer for this one since it's happening so soon after graduation. And I was honestly glad when Ashley told me that she would be heading this one up. She's the head of product development, so this entire line has been her first big project since coming on board with Pink Every Day. We each had several sets that we could send out to people, and then I've been working with the rest of the marketing team to line up the PR packages and early feedback from different creators and those in the beauty industry locally.

Being in the marketing department means I get to be a part of a little bit of everything with the company, from initial pitches to product development talks to production timelines to brand strategy to now early release prep. Product launches can take years before the line actually drops, and getting to be a part of the back end of that is so exciting. I may not know what order ingredients need to be listed in on the back of the moisturizer, but I do know how to pick colors for the packaging, the campaign, and the web pages to make sure this gets in front of the right people.

Tomorrow is the actual graduation ceremony, and then I get to start full-time at PED-CO next Tuesday. Pink Every Day Colorado is the official full company name, but we've started abbreviating it in internal communication and even in hashtags. We really do need to get some updated merch, nothing crazy, but I need a new water bottle. It might as well shout out what I get to do, because your girl has her first "big girl job" and she's going to absolutely kill it. And with me starting fully in my new role, that also means we have an incredibly packed week. There's a photo shoot meeting with Ashley and the photographer on Tuesday, a marketing planning meeting with the team on Wednesday, "family" packing day on Thursday, so we can get all the PR boxes packed and ready for shipping. And then Friday, we have a meeting with my dad and a handful of other investors and advisers as they review the next five-year plan of the company, including proposed product launches, non-profit collaborations, and employee and building growth. It's a lot, but we have so much we want to do as a business.

Jonathan: I picked up pizza for dinner tonight. The group is coming over so we can finish the planning for next week. Do you need anything, or are you all set?

> Me: All set. I'll be leaving the office in just a minute. I was just grabbing the last of the marketing materials that came in so I can make sure it's all good to go before next week.

Jonathan: Sounds good. See you soon.

Jonathan: Love you.

> Me: Love you too.

When I say "family" for the packing day – it really is just that. We have grown our own chosen family here, and I wouldn't trade this group for anyone. Sasha, the CEO of PED-CO, and her husband, Matt, get the group started. Then we have Matt's younger sister, Ashley, who was my roommate for a few semesters on campus, and she's engaged to Marcus, one of the marketing professors at CSU. Sasha's old roommate and best friend, Kylie, and her fiancé, Luca, are the next couple in the group. And then we have a few others that periodically jump in to help with the big projects. For tonight and for the family work day next week, Rowan (one of Marcus' previous students, he graduated last year) and my friend, and another old roommate, Corinne, will be joining us. It's probably going to be a loud and late night, but I wouldn't trade this group for anything. It's ours. And it's perfect.

"So, I know you said you didn't need a graduation present, but I got you something," Jonathan tells me at breakfast Sunday morning. We have to leave for the ceremony in about an hour, and I'm enjoying the later start to the morning after we finally called it a night around midnight last night. Not terribly late, but we tend to go to bed around ten most nights, at least during the school year. Once Shane and Henry are out for the summer, things are going to adjust a bit. Jonathan will have Fridays off from work so he can watch them on those days, while his parents have them on the others. They're not quite old enough to be home by themselves all day, and summer camps and programs are ridiculously expensive.

"I don't need anything, Jonathan. You really didn't have to do that." I practically pout at him. I'm still a bad gift receiver. I love gifting to other people, but I always feel a little weird when people give me things. It's not attached to any child trauma or weird previous interaction; it's just the thought of someone spending their time or energy or money on me when they probably could have been doing something for themselves. It feels weird.

"But it is something you need. And I needed to make the space at the shop, so if you think about it, you're helping me out." He stands and reaches for my hand, which I give him, a little hesitantly.

"Where are we going?" Although I think I know. We are heading to the front door, and I'm still in my slippers and pajamas. "I don't have a bra on yet, I can't go outside!" I pull my hand out of his and run to the bedroom real quick. I hear him laughing by the front door while I throw on a bra and T-shirt. I'll get on my cute grad dress when we come back inside. I do not get to go outside braless. Not comfortably anyway.

"Okay, I'm ready," I smile at him as I change my slippers for the sandals I keep by the front door.

"Alright, close your eyes, love." I make sure I'm lined up to not stub my toe on the door frame, and then close my eyes and let my husband lead me outside. When he finally lets me open them, I see the most beautiful car in the driveway. Complete with a huge sparkly pink bow on the hood.

"Jonathan! It's so pretty! Oh, you're right, I needed a new car! Isn't this one of the ones you were working on for Dad from the auction, though?" Don't ask me for any specs on this thing besides the fact that it has four doors and is a beautiful light blue color – not quite Robin's Egg or Sky Blue, almost like a light slate blue if I had to call it anything. It's the size of an SUV, but definitely prettier than anything I was looking at while perusing used car online sales over the last month. Guess I wasn't as subtle as I thought when looking. I've been wanting something bigger, especially when I have to transport products or props for a photo shoot.

"Nope, this is one I bought and it's been hiding in one of the bays at the shop until today. Do you want to know what it is, or do you want to go sit in it so you can name her?"

I pop up on my tiptoes so I can kiss his cheek.

"You know me so well."

Sitting in this car is an experience. It doesn't quite have that new car smell. He must have taken it to a car wash or detailed the interior himself so it wouldn't smell like all the chemicals used at the shop. I take a moment to adjust the mirrors, look at what's on the dashboard, and play with the settings just a bit.

"So, what's her name?" Jonathan opens the passenger door and sits down next to me. I love the space in here. I could probably sit on his lap for some garage "activities" if we leaned the passenger seat back just a little bit. Nope, we do not have time for that this morning. Bummer.

"Maddie," I say with all the confidence that I can muster. I knew it the moment I saw her sitting in the driveway.

"S.J. Tilly again, right?" He seems so proud of himself for knowing that, and I lean over to kiss him right on the lips.

"You really are the perfect book boyfriend."

"Well, I saw it at one of the shows earlier this year, and I knew it was yours. I just had to find the perfect color and the right extras that you would need. I knew you would find the perfect name for her. But she suits you."

"She really is so pretty." I look over my car one more time before I step out, so we can get ready for my graduation.

"She's the ride for you."

"That's so insanely cheesy, but I love it." And then he's chasing me inside so he can try to tickle me in retaliation for calling him cheesy.

Chapter Thirty-Two

TILLY

STRAWBERRY THYME SUN TEA

Social Post: Photo shoot for the new product launch is today. I can't wait to share more about what we've been working on at Pink Every Day! I get to be behind the scenes today so I'm ready with multiple pens, water bottles, and lip balm. #photoshootday #pinkeveryday #marketingthings #productlaunchprep

Image Description: Bag filled with my photo shoot essentials — snacks, water bottles, gum, mints, lip balms, etc.

It's photo shoot day!! While Ashley was the main one planning this, I am so excited that it's finally here. All the models are meeting us at the studio where we will be shooting, so I just need to grab my kit that's already packed and ready at the dining room table, and we will be on our way. I have several bags and products already loaded in the back of my car that we will need to utilize for the day. So I'm glad that Jonathan requested to go with me so he could help bring things inside and run to get anything that might pop up during the shoot. As long as I can still drive, fine. I may be slightly obsessed with my new ride. It's a Mercedes, and it's new, and that's really all I know about it. The guys all totally geeked out over it when we got together last week, though, so that was fun.

The studio today is set up in a mix of spaces. We have a bathroom counter set up, a work desk area, a cozy living space, and a smaller dorm room vibe type area. When we arrive, I see they've made a few other adjustments that we hadn't talked about.

"Babe, can you bring the rest of the boxes inside while I go find Ashley? This isn't what was discussed in our last meeting, and I need to make sure she has a handle on things before the models get here. We've only rented the space for today, and if we need to rework things, it's going to cut into our shoot time, and then we are going to need to refigure the shoot list." My mind is running a million directions, and I'm trying to categorize them in a way that's manageable before I have a full anxiety attack. Kind of hard to do without my notebook in front of me. Why did I put that in my bag and not my purse? I need paper.

Jonathan must sense my internal meltdown because he pulls me close, holding both of my hands in his own, centering me so I'm looking at his eyes, his face, and not the people moving around behind me. Probably setting up another unapproved backdrop. Why on earth would we need a wood shop for today? Ridiculous.

"I'll bring stuff inside. Take a breath. You have a role to complete today, and everyone else does too. Trust your team. Control what you can."

"And leave the rest." I take a deep breath, matching the movement of my husband. He's right. It's okay. We have a plan, and we can pivot if needed.

"I do need to find Ashley, though, it looks like we're going to have to adjust what we're shooting and when, based on the lighting in the front setups. I don't think we were planning on having the natural light on those backdrops, and I need to know what the updated plan for the day is."

He places a quick kiss on my forehead and then releases my

hands so I can run off to find her. After peaking in several rooms, this place is absolutely massive, I finally find her talking to the photographer as they look over the shoot list we finalized yesterday.

The papers are all over the table, divided among the models, products, and backdrops. Only, this is the first time that I'm seeing the model photos paired up with each of the "chapters" of the story we are shooting today. And I quickly notice a few things. First, all of the models are male – which, honestly, I'm stoked about. Men need good skincare too! Second, I know every single man who is photographed. One of them is my husband. What? I go to look a bit closer to confirm, and yep, that's Jonathan. I'm still trying to fully digest what I'm seeing when I hear a familiar voice entering the room behind me.

"There you are, Tilly. Are you ready for today?"

"When did you add being a model to your already very impressive resume, Dad?"

Apparently, Jonathan has been planning this since our wedding day (the second one) with Ashley. When we had talked about skincare and wanting to make sure it was shown as something for every person for every day, I had brought up that I would like to see a broader demographic of male models showing off products like these. I've seen some male models in skincare campaigns before, but they are all obviously models and usually in the eighteen to forty age range.

Now that I get to see the entire campaign story, this really is perfect. It combines my original thoughts with the practicality of everyday lives of, well, regular guys. And each setup aligns with the men who are here today. Matt is going to be showing off the blue screen benefits of the moisturizer, as well as the setting spray we launched last year. He is in a computer-based field, so it's perfect for him. Marcus is going to be in a library setting, showing off the anti-aging and early-mature skin benefits of the line. He's in his late thirties, so not technically "mature" yet, but a lot of skincare is proactive.

Luca has two sets. The first is in a setting that looks a lot like his woodworker shop to show off the need for a heavy-duty moisturizer when working in dryer climates and conditions. His second one is going to be fun. We are doing his makeup in full glam to show how long-lasting the setting spray and powder work when used in conjunction with a solid skin prep routine. Even when dancing all night under studio lights. He does competitive West Coast Swing dancing with Kylie. And while they rarely do full glam, there are instances where he does wear some makeup for promotional campaigns for the dance studio.

My dad, Jonathan's dad, Jonathan's brother-in-law, and Matt's dad are set up in a board room and an office setup. They're all white-collar workers, so this is perfect for them. And all of the dads are in their sixties, so we will be able to show the mature skin benefits on them. And Jonathan's brother-in-law will be showing the travel sizes for ease of use when traveling for work.

Jonathan is going to be doing the unboxing videos and the detail shots since he's the most familiar with the product already. He's also doing a few styled shots showing the importance of skincare in the cold and dry seasons. And the last set is with Rowan – a mini coffee shop setup with a variety of coffees and teas behind him, along with an espresso machine, mini juicer, and even a cold brew pitcher. Because having steam on the face all day isn't actually great for you, good skincare helps, though.

Ashley and Jonathan really did think of everything. Adding in the bathroom sets, the unboxing and packaging videos, and the how-to photo shots on a few different faces – this is going to be perfect. This is going to be incredible.

"I can't believe you have all agreed to this! Thank you so, so much! I can't wait to see it all come together." I tell everyone gathered in the main space before we break off to the first rotation. The two photographers we originally planned on are now a team of five. Each of the team members here is in charge of one group of models, so we can stay on pace. With nine models and eight hours to shoot, set, prep, and shoot again – it's going to be a very full day.

"We've seen the work you have all put into this over the last five years, now we get to do something practical to help you with this next launch. You built Pink Every Day, and we get to be the cheerleaders behind the incredible women that make this happen each and every day." Matt's dad responds to me, looking at his daughter, his daughter-in-law, and me as he talks. He looks over at Kylie, too, making sure she gets the recognition of his words. She may not be on staff with us, but she has a big part in a lot of the campaigns, and she designed most of the offices for us, too. She's been there for photo shoots, campaign planning meetings, and all the girls' lunches as we brainstorm what's coming next.

I don't miss the tears in many eyes as we all just take a moment to look around. Five years ago, this was one influencer looking to grow her platform. Now, we are a full company making a difference in our community.

And I wouldn't ask for anything more.
Because this, right here, is our happily ever after.

The end.

13

• June

• Wednesday

2:00 *tail light replacement*

165-201

• Week 24

Epilogue

JONATHAN

"How do you feel about a group getaway?" I'm working on some things at home while Tilly does the same. We've been married (the second time) for four years now, and being her husband is still my greatest accomplishment and privilege. Life hasn't really gotten slower at all, but it's at a place where we can make plans for vacations and trips. It helps that the boys are old enough to get themselves on the bus in the mornings.

"That could be fun, what are you all thinking?" Tilly closes her laptop, logging off for the day. I love that we have days where we get to work from home together, but it's definitely very easy to work until bedtime if we aren't careful. We both love what we do. Which is another reason that a vacation is probably very overdue.

"I was talking with Matt and Luca, and we're thinking about a cabin trip after the new year. Wait until the college kids are back in classes so there's not too much traffic in the tourist spots. We'd

invite Marcus and Ashley too, of course. But just the eight of us, a cabin up in Estes or something like that, and a few days to unplug and rest. There isn't a new Pink Every Day launch until June, so this is the perfect time to get away."

She nods and hums in approval as I go through what we've been thinking about. "I think a few days away will be perfect. Corinne is coming back to town in the next few weeks too, so I need to set up a time to get lunch with her. But that's really the only thing on my agenda over the next few weeks."

"I'll let the guys know and we'll start planning it."

"Why can't the girls plan it?" She pouts at me and I have to laugh. She still knows I can barely tell her 'no' when she gives me that face. But it's not going to work this time.

"Because we already have some things lined up. And we want to spoil our girls for a few days. Which will go a lot better if you let us surprise you and aren't worrying about schedules and reservations and details." I playfully remind her, walking over to her chair so I can boop her on the nose real quick before I kiss the top of her head. "Let's go to bed, love. We both have long days tomorrow and have a vacation to plan."

"Sometimes I wish I didn't tell you that I liked surprises. You do them way too often."

"What can I say? I enjoy spoiling my girl. I'll make sure you know the dates as soon as we get the cabin reserved. Leave the rest to me."

THE MAKEUP AND MOCHAS SERIES IS OFFICIALLY DONE!

WELL, ALMOST...

Be watching Nikki's socials and her website to be the first to hear about two upcoming spin-off projects from this series, as well as announcements for upcoming releases, events, and promotions. Thank you for being a part of Pink Every Day and the Makeup and Mochas series.

Want to get involved? The pinkeverydayco.com site is now under construction. Submit women-owned businesses and organizations that give back to local communities on the website. Over the coming months, ways that you can get involved in supporting similar organizations will be shared on the site. While this series has been cozy fiction, Pink Every Day has become a little passion project that is now coming to reality. For now, it's starting with highlighting the businesses and people who are putting in the work, just like Sasha and the incredible women we met in this series. Where will it go from here? Not sure. It's still in chapter one.

OTHER BOOKS BY NIKKI GRANT

ROMANCE NOVELS:

MAKEUP AND MOCHAS SERIES

The Funnel to You
The Man for You
The Dance for You
The Ride for You
My Kind of Slay (Winter 2025)

THRILLER NOVELS:
Our Journeys to Love (Winter 2025)

Check nikkigrantwrites.com for other updates on future projects.

ACKNOWLEDGEMENTS

While the previous books in this series have been heavy in their own ways, I knew this one would carry a different type of lightness. This was my love letter to romance novels and I got to just enjoy the sweetness of the story. Even with the bits of drama, this one concluded a lot of the pieces of Makeup and Mochas – as well as hinting towards what's to come with future projects. Did you catch them?

To my husband, thank you for being my perfect book boyfriend. And even though I'm a horrible road trip partner, thank you for letting me enjoy being a passenger princess every time and for cheering me on for those random trips that I request to drive.

Naughty Nook PR and Grace Farnsworth, thank you for your help in promotion and sharing the entire series with the book community.

Avery's Modern Teahouse – thank you for all you are doing in our local community. I can't wait to see what good comes from the work you do each and every day!

Charly – this series vision was so perfectly done on each and every page. I love how it all came together and appreciate all that you did in the course of this design process.

Chris and Joey – the model photos for this book are stunning! Thanks for helping narrow it down each and every time for me and giving me the perfect "book boyfriend" for every title.

Mekhala – Thank you for helping me get this story all polished and pretty as we got ready for publication. I loved all your notes as you read and helping me to become a better writer through these pages.

My beta readers and street team members: Daisy, Mackenzey, Teia, Cici, Amy, Ely, Alyssa, Tori, Kitty, Lauren, Jan, Janna, Rachel, Tea, Jennifer, Tiffani, Jamie, Katie, and Alison – each of you have such an important part of this story and I appreciate the feedback, input, and conversations we get to have while I'm drafting. This series wouldn't be here without you.

S.J. Tilly – thank you for showing me that plus size bodies don't have to hide in romance novels. That we can be loved, loud, and excited to be seen. Your books continue to be some of my favorites and I love that I got to showcase a few of those in this story.

And yes, reader, if you haven't checked out Brightside Candles yet – please do. Their editions are some of the prettiest I have ever seen and the quality is incredible!